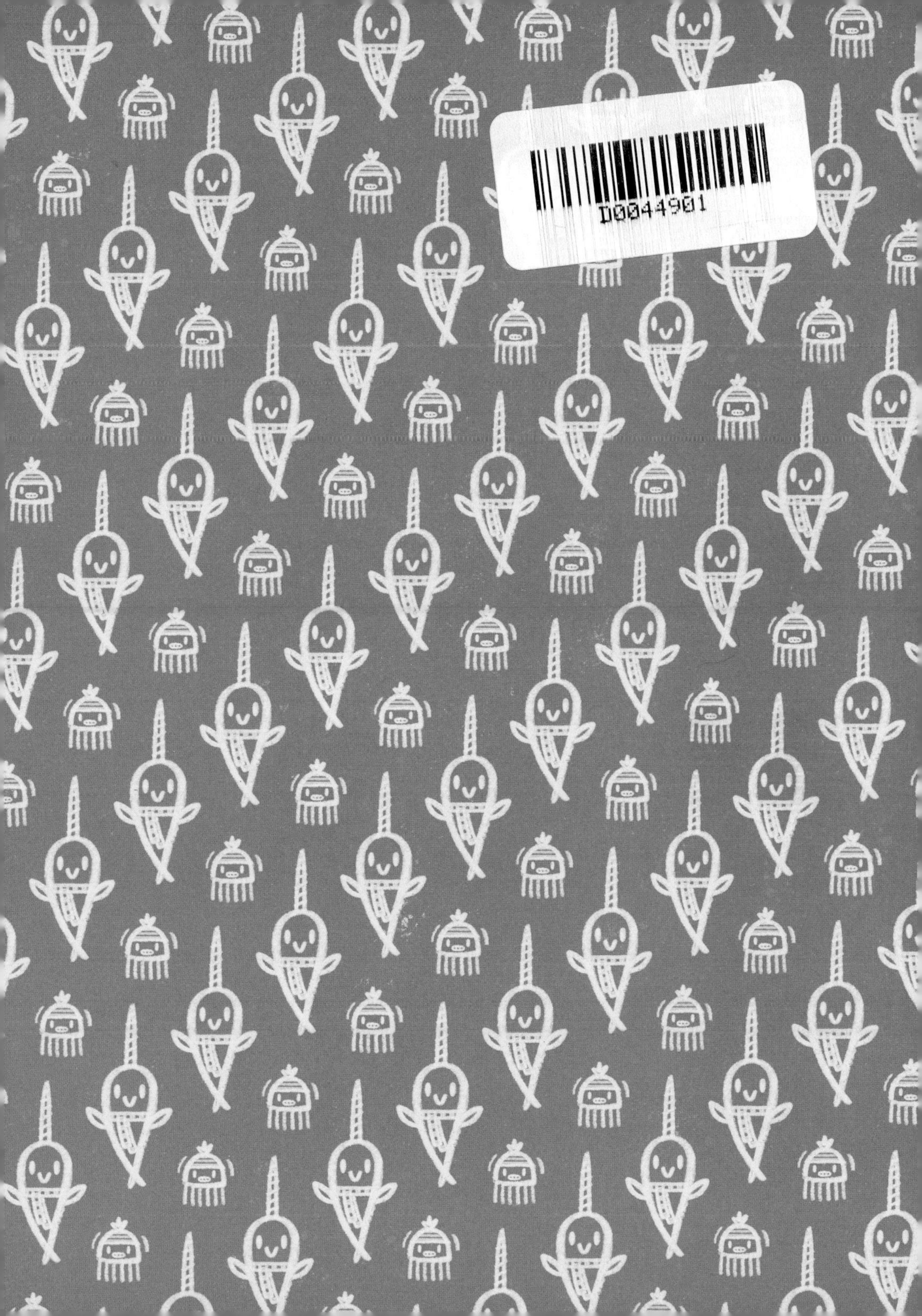

HAVE YOU READ THESE
NARWHAL AND JELLY BOOKS?

NARWHAL: UNICORN OF THE SEA!

SUPER NARWHAL AND JELLY JOLT

PEANUT BUTTER AND JELLY

NARWHAL'S OTTER FRIEND

HAPPY NARWHALIDAYS

BEN CLANTON

tundra

TO GWEN! IT IS A GIFT TO BE YOUR PAPA!

Text and illustrations copyright © 2020 by Ben Clanton

Tundra Books, an imprint of Penguin Random House Canada Young Readers, a Penguin Random House Company

All rights reserved. The use of any part of this publication reproduced, transmitted in any form or by any means, electronic, mechanical, photocopying, recording, or otherwise, or stored in a retrieval system, without the prior written consent of the publisher — or, in case of photocopying or other reprographic copying, a licence from the Canadian Copyright Licensing Agency — is an infringement of the copyright law.

Library and Archives Canada Cataloguing in Publication

Title: Happy narwhalidays / Ben Clanton.
Names: Clanton, Ben, 1988- author, illustrator.
Series: Clanton, Ben, 1988- Narwhal and Jelly book.
Description: Series statement: A Narwhal and Jelly book ; 5
Identifiers: Canadiana (print) 20190237015 | Canadiana (ebook) 20190237031 |
ISBN 9780735262515 (hardcover) | ISBN 9780735262539 (EPUB)
Subjects: LCGFT: Graphic novels.
Classification: LCC PZ7.C523 Hap 2020 | DDC j741.5/973—dc23

Published simultaneously in the United States of America by Tundra Books of Northern New York,
an imprint of Penguin Random House Canada Young Readers, a Penguin Random House Company

Library of Congress Control Number: 2019955874

Edited by Tara Walker and Peter Phillips
Designed by Ben Clanton
The artwork in this book was rendered in colored pencil, watercolor and ink, and colored digitally.
The text was set in a typeface based on hand lettering by Ben Clanton.

Photos: (sphere glass ball) © Beautyimage/Shutterstock; (ice cream scoop) © Sompoch Tangthai/Shutterstock;
(butterfly) © Boule/Shutterstock; (sugar cone) © Leeyakorn06/Shutterstock; (jelly bean) © Dan Kosmayer/
Shutterstock; (book) © Billion Photos/Shutterstock; (corn cob) © AminaAster/Shutterstock;
(strawberry) © Valentina Razumova/Shutterstock; (waffle) © Tiger Images/Shutterstock

Printed and bound in China

www.penguinrandomhouse.ca

3 4 5   24 23 22 21

CONTENTS

JINGLE SHELLS, JINGLE SHELLS, JINGLE ALL THE WAY!

WHILE SWIMMING IN THE BAY! OH WHAT FUN IT IS TO SING

JINGLE SHELLS, JINGLE SHELLS, JINGLE ALL THE WAY!

'TIS THE SEASON

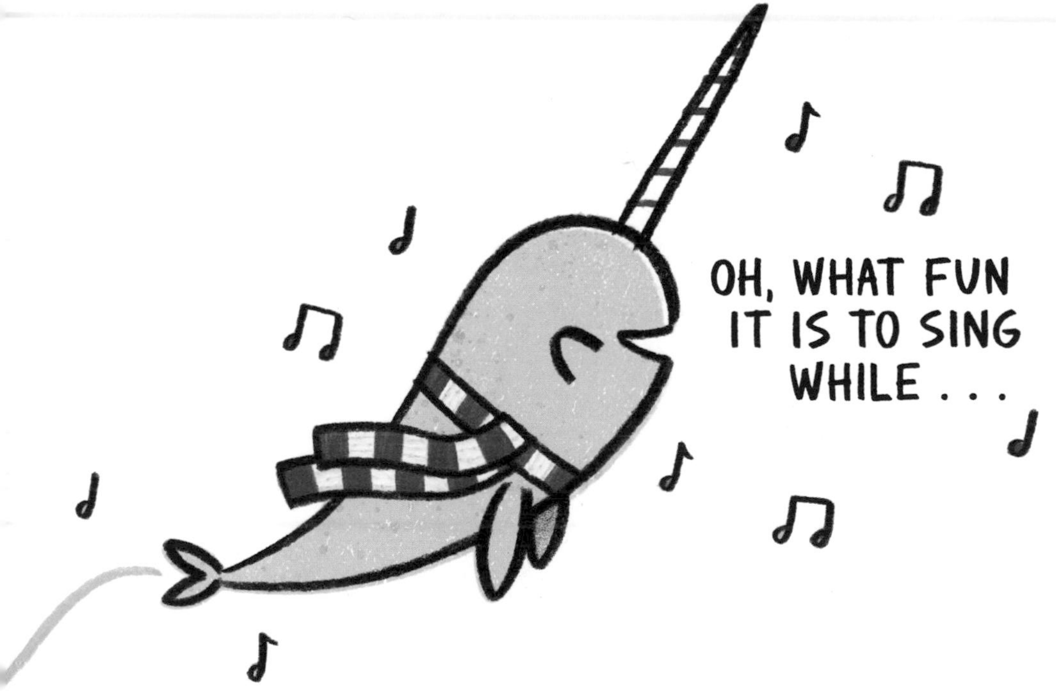
OH, WHAT FUN IT IS TO SING WHILE . . .

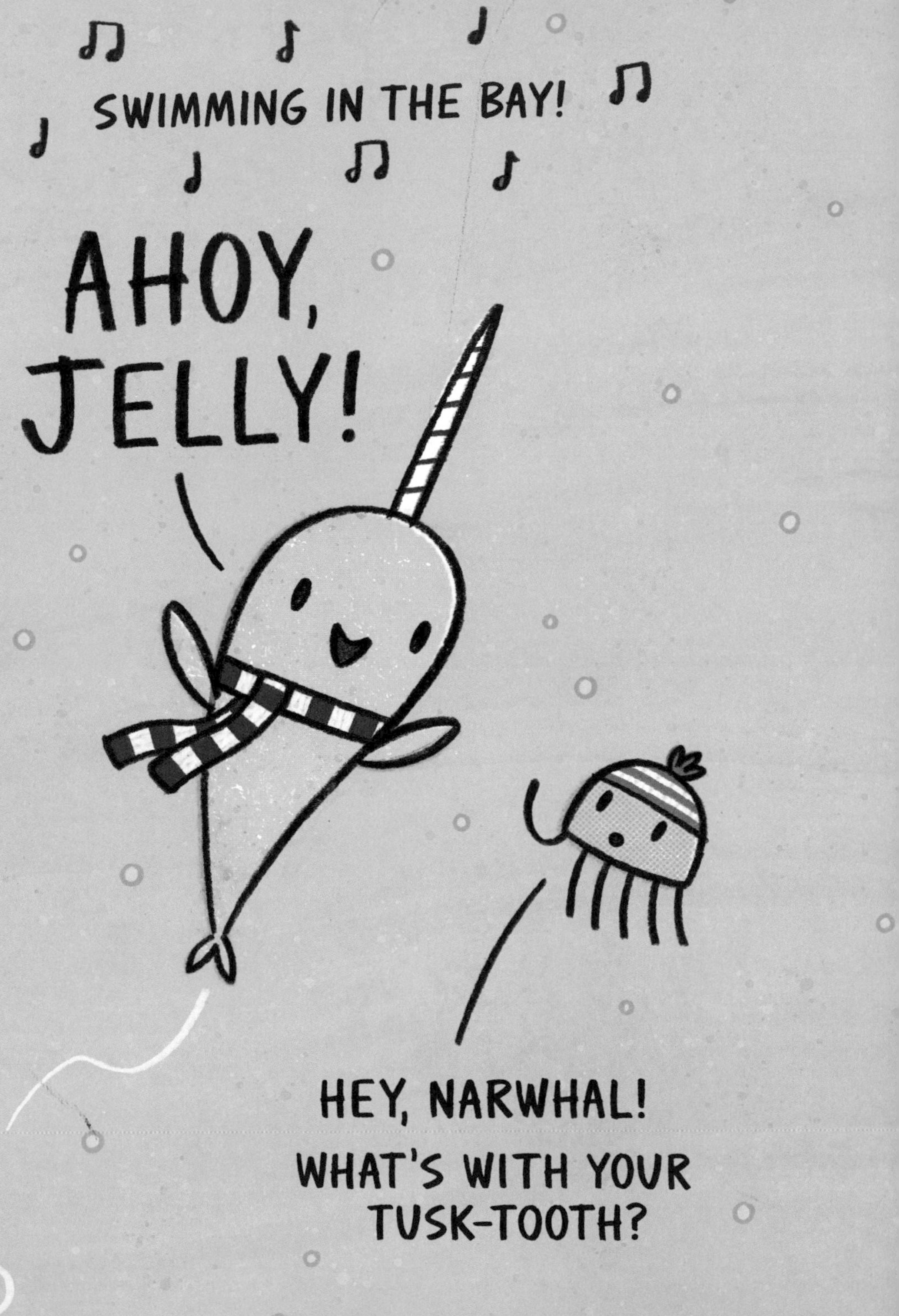
SWIMMING IN THE BAY!
AHOY, JELLY!
HEY, NARWHAL!
WHAT'S WITH YOUR TUSK-TOOTH?

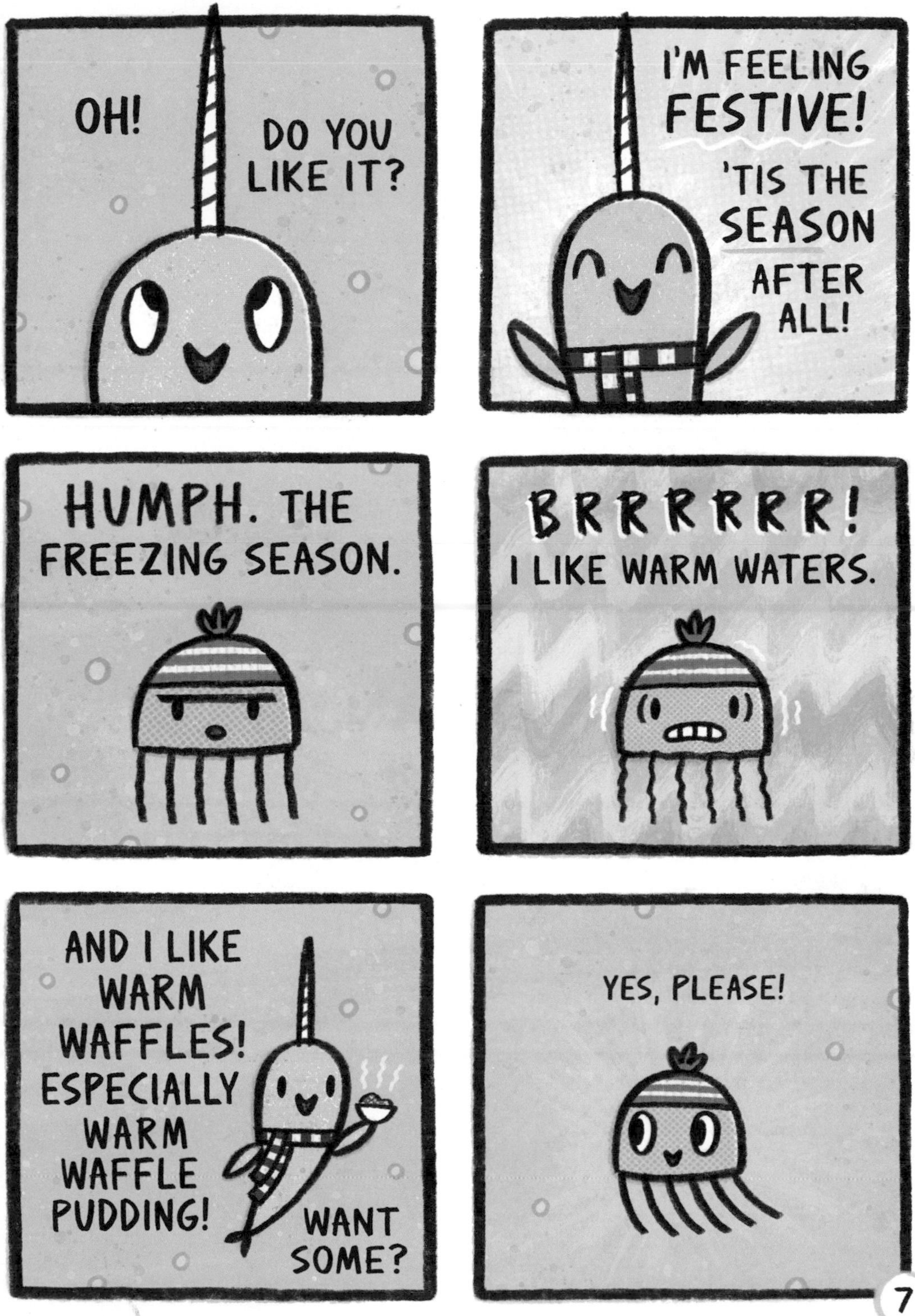
OH!
DO YOU LIKE IT?
I'M FEELING FESTIVE!
'TIS THE SEASON AFTER ALL!
HUMPH. THE FREEZING SEASON.
BRRRRRR!
I LIKE WARM WATERS.
AND I LIKE WARM WAFFLES! ESPECIALLY WARM WAFFLE PUDDING!
WANT SOME?
YES, PLEASE!

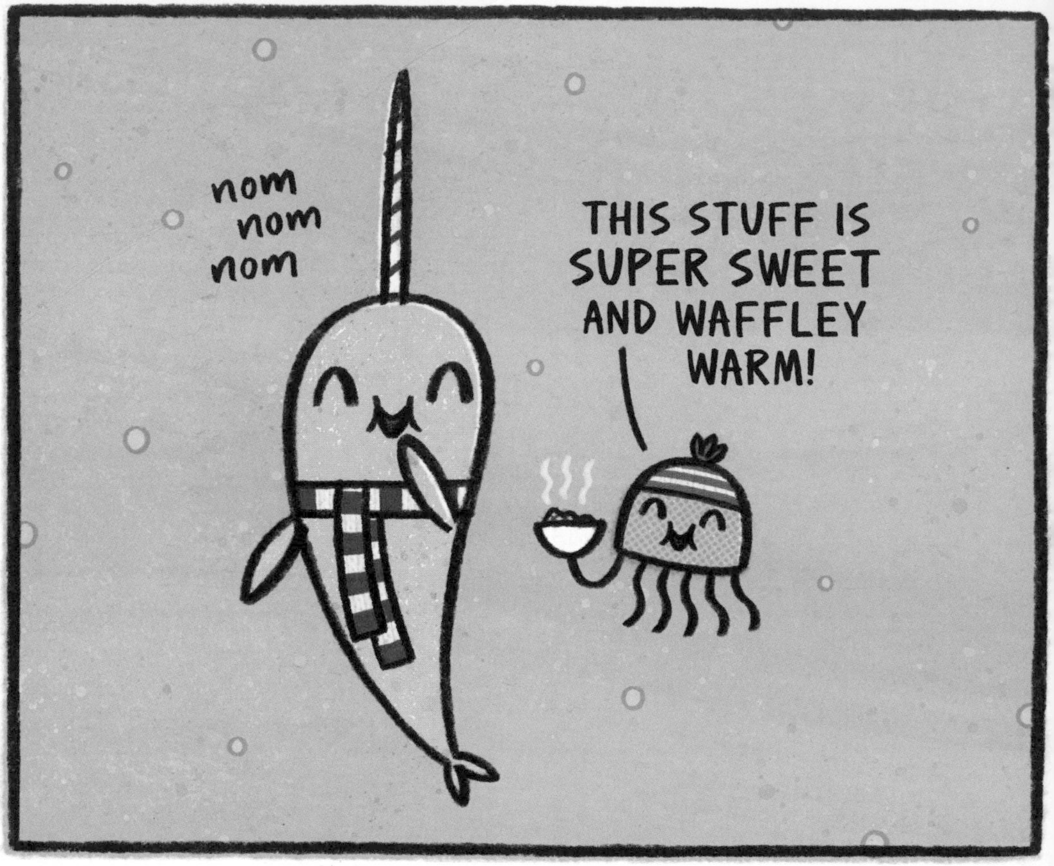
nom nom nom
THIS STUFF IS SUPER SWEET AND WAFFLEY WARM!

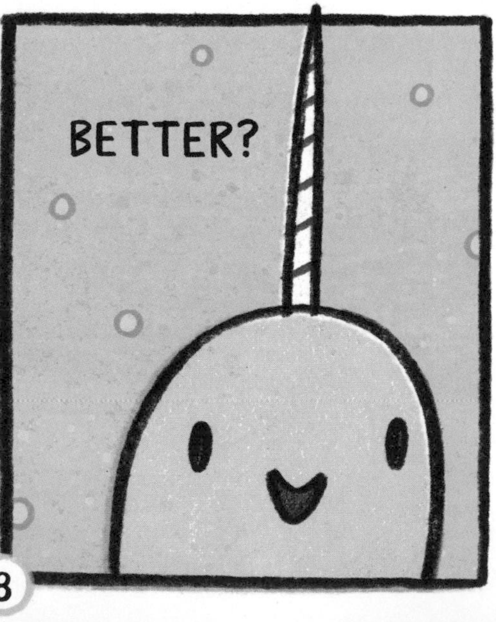
BETTER?

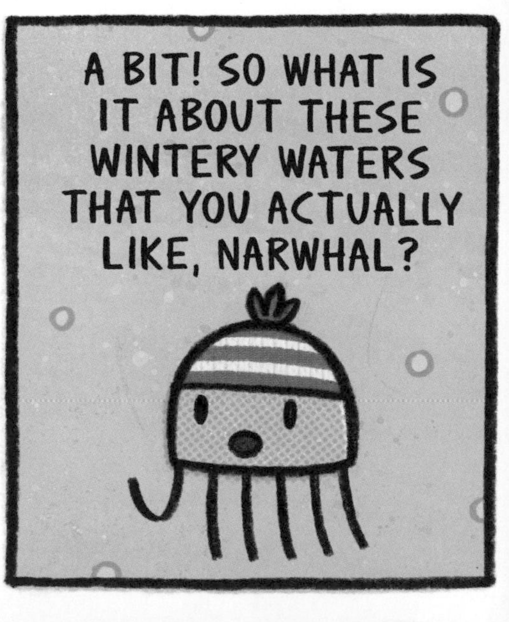
A BIT! SO WHAT IS IT ABOUT THESE WINTERY WATERS THAT YOU ACTUALLY LIKE, NARWHAL?

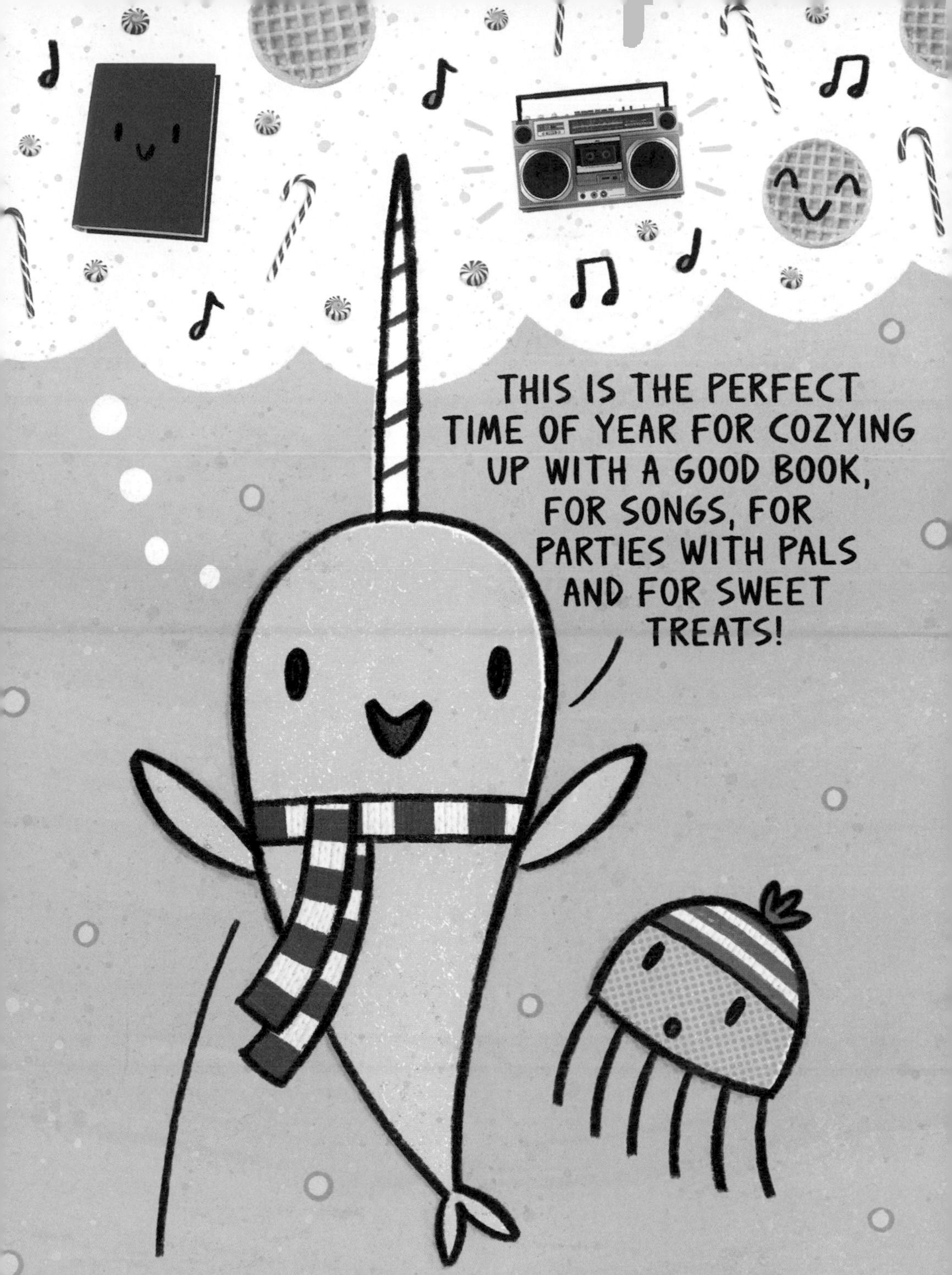
THIS IS THE PERFECT TIME OF YEAR FOR COZYING UP WITH A GOOD BOOK, FOR SONGS, FOR PARTIES WITH PALS AND FOR SWEET TREATS!

ALSO, THIS IS THE TIME OF YEAR WHEN . . .

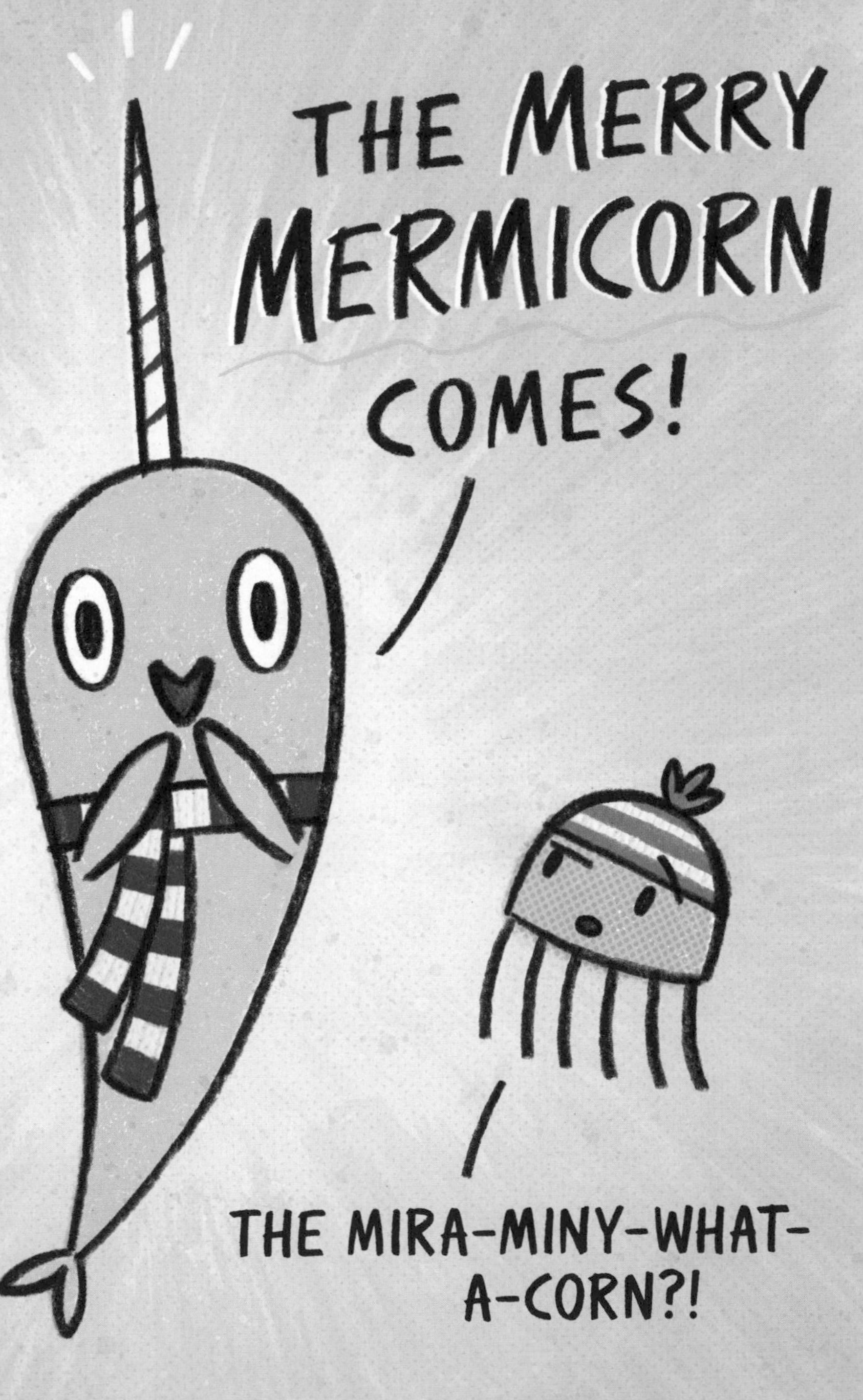
THE MERRY MERMICORN COMES!
THE MIRA-MINY-WHAT-A-CORN?!

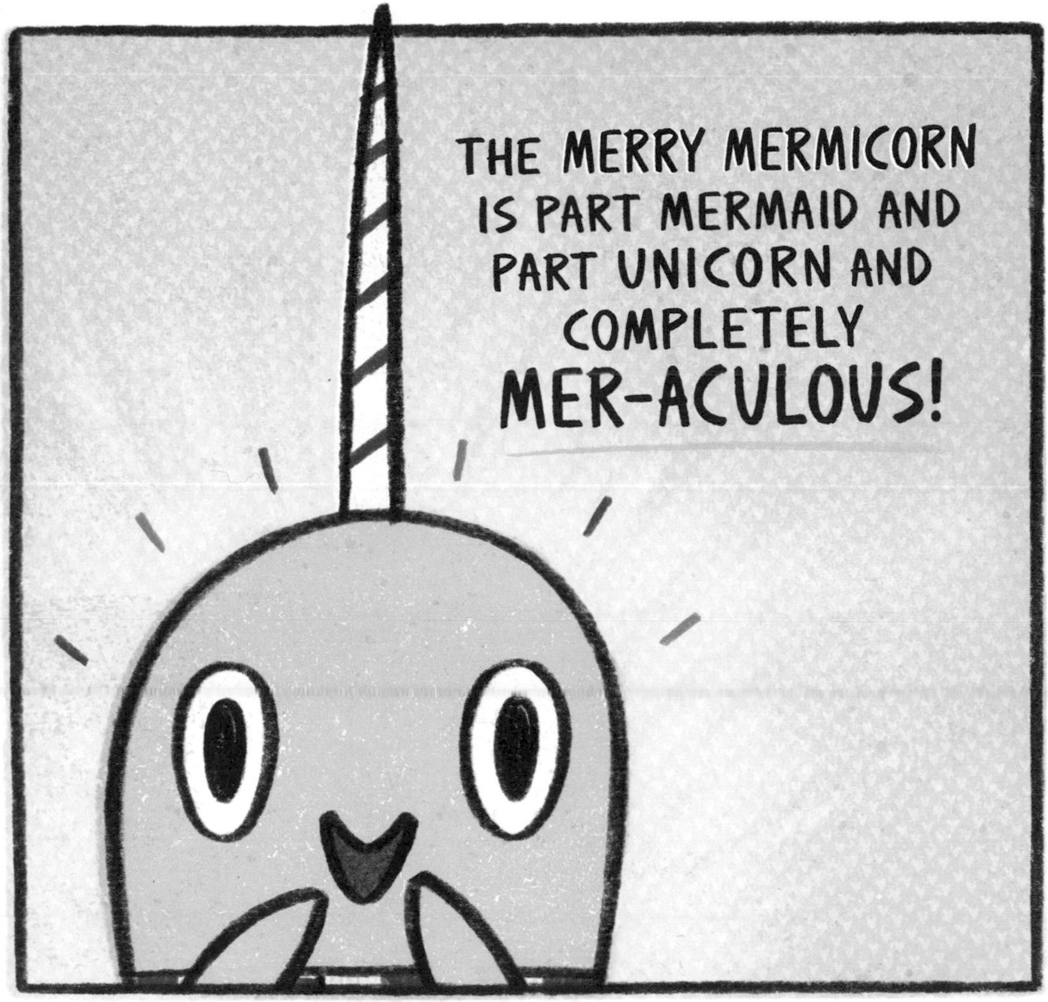
THE MERRY MERMICORN IS PART MERMAID AND PART UNICORN AND COMPLETELY MER-ACULOUS!

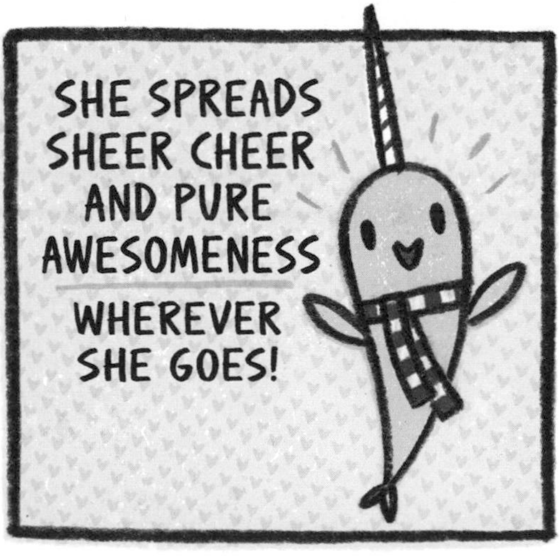
SHE SPREADS SHEER CHEER AND PURE AWESOMENESS WHEREVER SHE GOES!

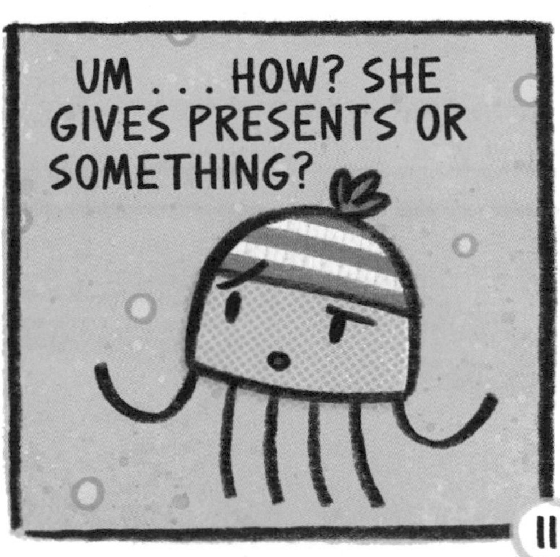
UM . . . HOW? SHE GIVES PRESENTS OR SOMETHING?

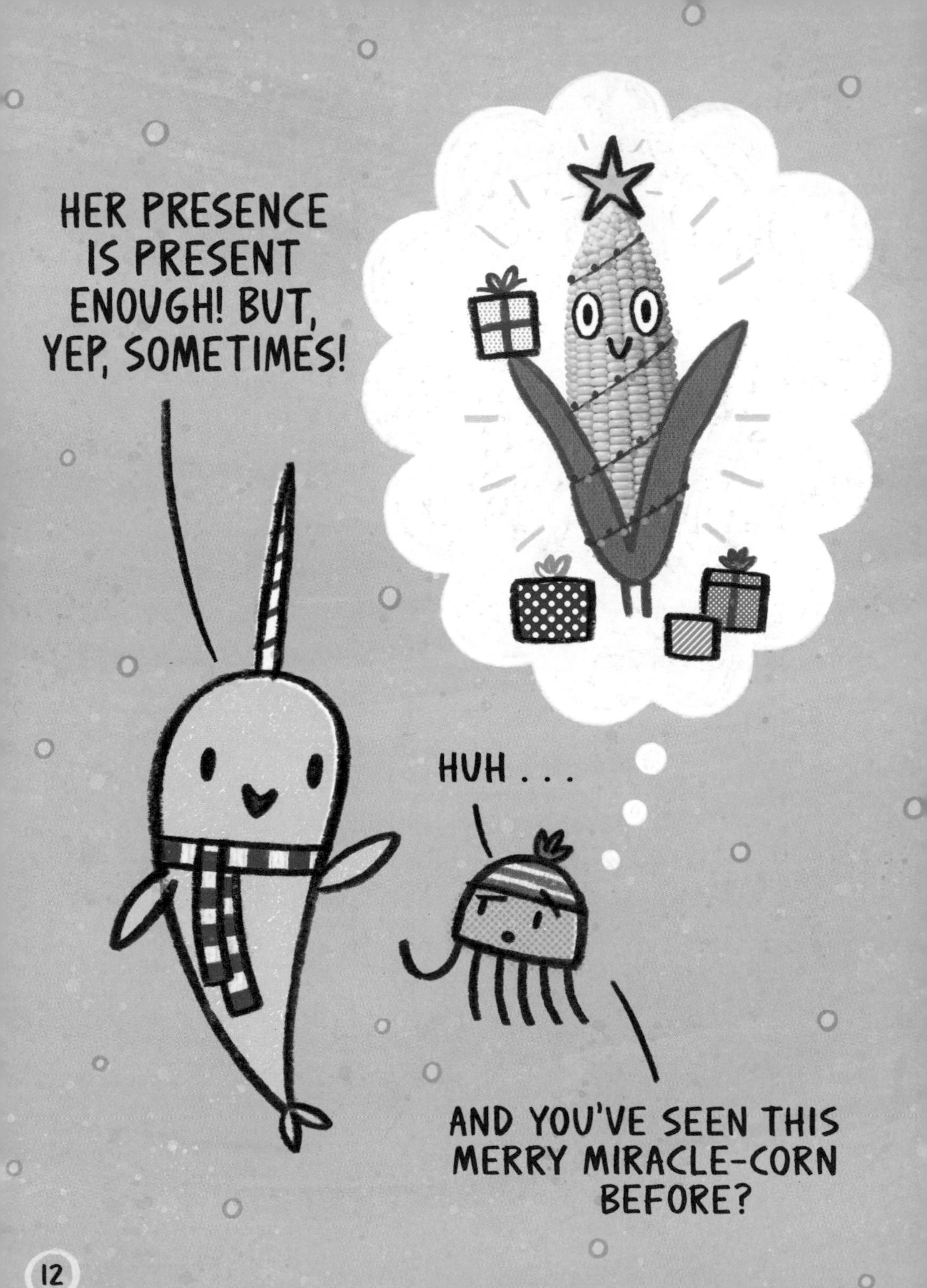
HER PRESENCE IS PRESENT ENOUGH! BUT, YEP, SOMETIMES!
HUH . . .
AND YOU'VE SEEN THIS MERRY MIRACLE-CORN BEFORE?

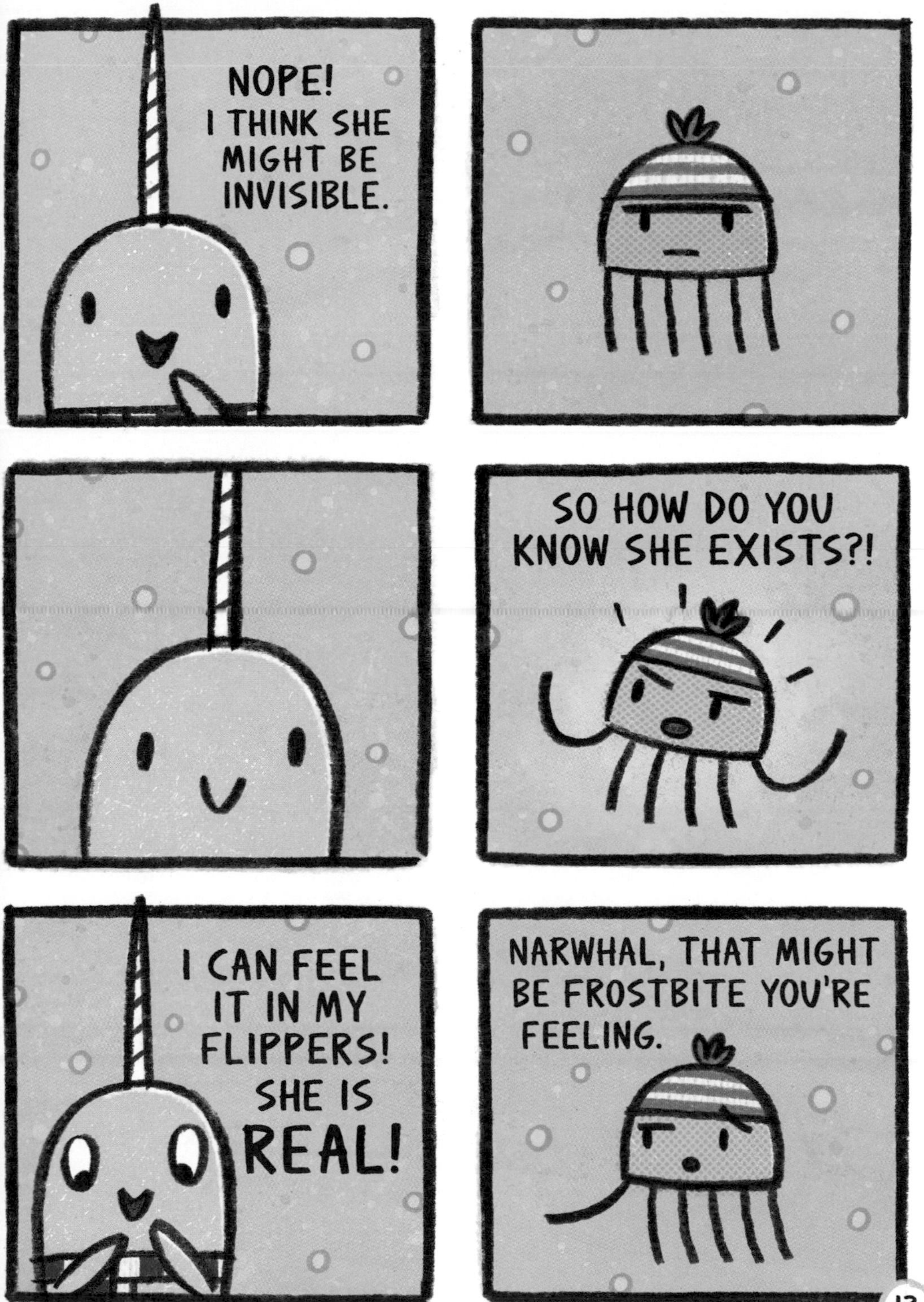
NOPE! I THINK SHE MIGHT BE INVISIBLE.
SO HOW DO YOU KNOW SHE EXISTS?!
I CAN FEEL IT IN MY FLIPPERS! SHE IS REAL!
NARWHAL, THAT MIGHT BE FROSTBITE YOU'RE FEELING.

DO YOU REMEMBER WHEN WE MET? HOW I THOUGHT **YOU** WERE IMAGINARY?

YEP! AND I THOUGHT YOU MUST BE MY IMAGINARY FRIEND!

RIGHT. SINCE THEN IT'S BECOME PRETTY CLEAR YOU'RE ACTUALLY REAL. SHARK SEES YOU. TURTLE SEES YOU. MR. BLOWFISH . . . EVERYONE! SO UNLESS EVERYONE ELSE IS ALSO IMAGINING YOU, OR I'M IMAGINING EVERYONE ELSE IS IMAGINING YOU, YOU <u>ARE</u> REAL.

THIS MERRY CORN . . . NOT SO MUCH. NOT A CHANCE!

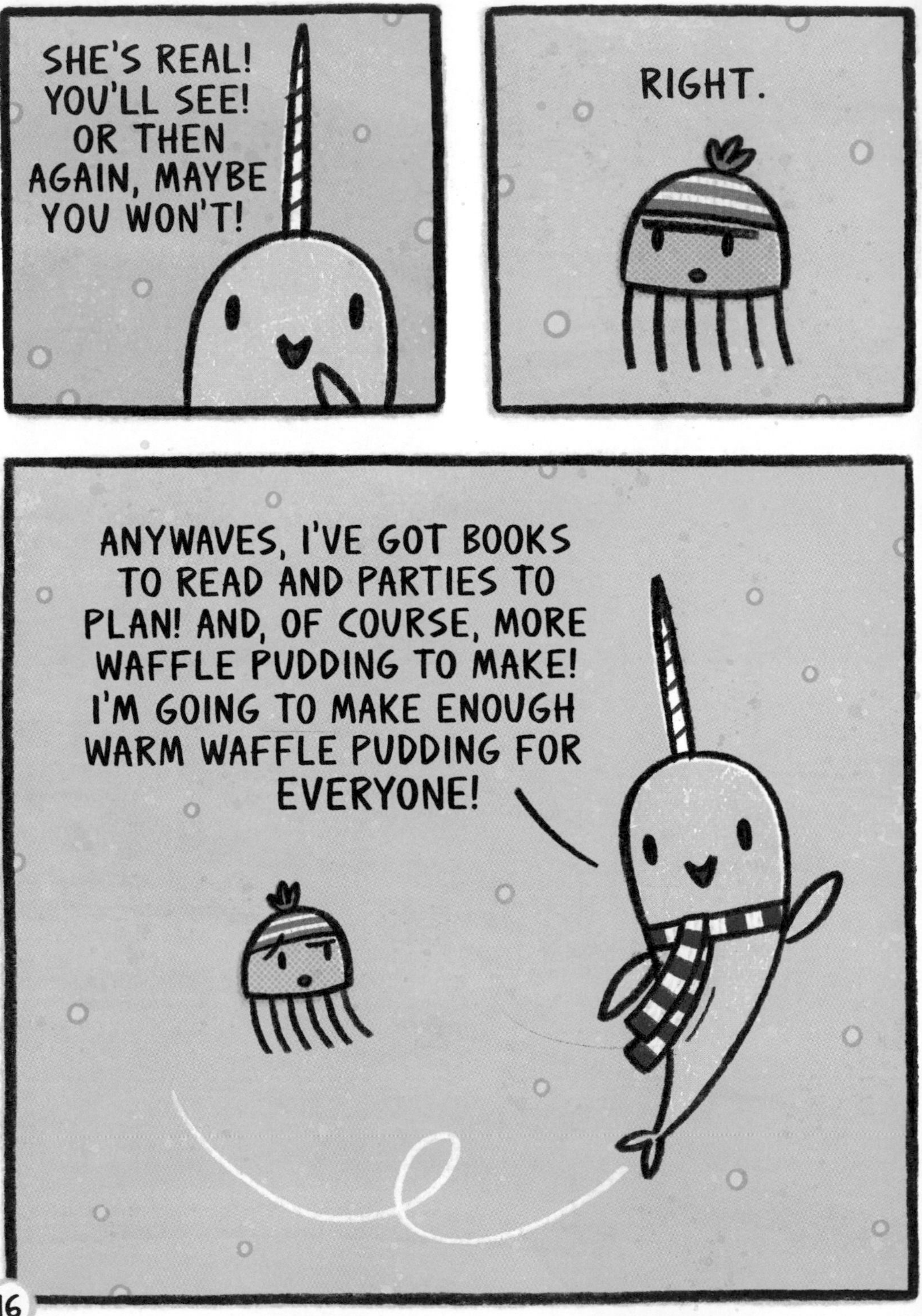
SHE'S REAL! YOU'LL SEE! OR THEN AGAIN, MAYBE YOU WON'T!
RIGHT.
ANYWAVES, I'VE GOT BOOKS TO READ AND PARTIES TO PLAN! AND, OF COURSE, MORE WAFFLE PUDDING TO MAKE! I'M GOING TO MAKE ENOUGH WARM WAFFLE PUDDING FOR EVERYONE!

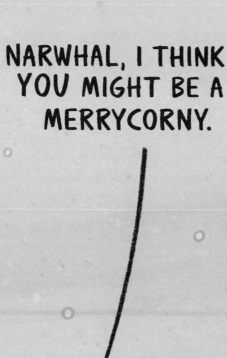

NARWHAL, I THINK YOU MIGHT BE A MERRYCORNY.

AWWW, THANKS, JELLY! SEE YOU IN A BIT! ENJOY THESE WONDERFUL WATERS!

JINGLE SHELLS, JINGLE SHELLS, JINGLE ALL THE WAY!

HUMPH-BUG.

COOL FACTS

NARWHALS LIVE IN THE COLD ARCTIC OCEAN. A FATTY TISSUE CALLED BLUBBER KEEPS THEM WARM. BLUBBER MAKES UP MORE THAN A THIRD OF A NARWHAL'S WEIGHT.

BLUBBER! THAT IS A FUN WORD TO SAY!

BLUBBER! BLUBBER! BLUBBER!

TIME FOR A TRIP TO THE TROPICS!

JELLYFISH CAN BE FOUND IN ALL SORTS OF WATERS. SOME LIVE IN THE COLD ARCTIC WATERS AND OTHERS LIVE IN WARM TROPICAL WATERS.

WE CAN BEAR ALMOST ANYTHING!

TARDIGRADES, COMMONLY KNOWN AS WATER BEARS, ARE WATER-DWELLING MICRO-ANIMALS THAT CAN SURVIVE IN TEMPERATURES AS HOT AS 304°F (151°C) AND AS COLD AS ABSOLUTE ZERO.

MORE COOL FACTS

NICE!

SNOW UNDERWATER? MARINE SNOW IS ACTUALLY A SHOWER OF MOSTLY ORGANIC MATERIAL FALLING FROM THE UPPER WATERS OF THE OCEAN.

GREENLAND SHARKS, WHICH CAN LIVE FOR POSSIBLY 400 YEARS, PREFER COLD WATERS. DURING WINTER, THEY MIGRATE TO THE SURFACE LAYER, WHICH IS COLDER THAN THE SEA FLOOR AT THAT TIME OF YEAR.

WE'RE COLD-BLOODED!

CUDDLE-HUDDLE TIME!

EMPEROR PENGUINS HUDDLE TOGETHER TO KEEP FROM FREEZING.

DENSE, LAYERED FEATHERS AND INSULATING FAT ARE VITAL TO PENGUINS' SURVIVAL.

THE PERFECT PRESENT

A LITTLE WHILE LATER, WHEN TRYING TO FIND SOME WARMER WATERS . . .

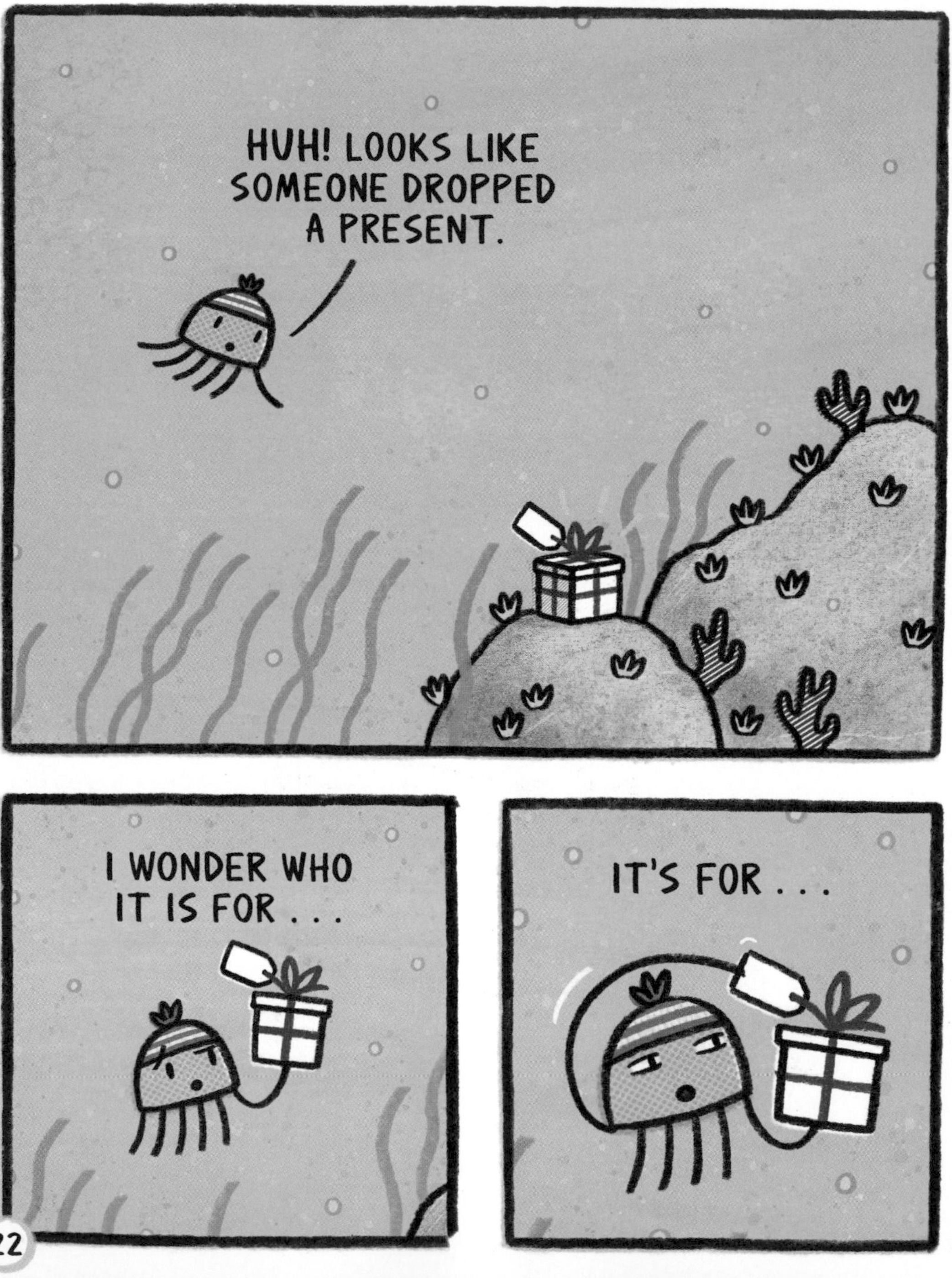
HUH! LOOKS LIKE SOMEONE DROPPED A PRESENT.
I WONDER WHO IT IS FOR . . .
IT'S FOR . . .

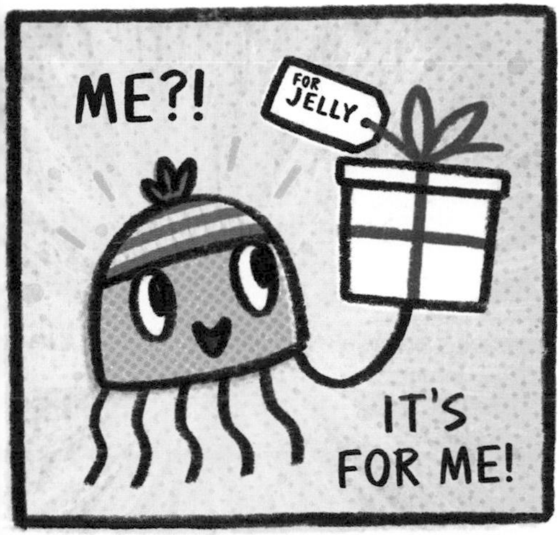
ME?!
FOR JELLY
IT'S FOR ME!

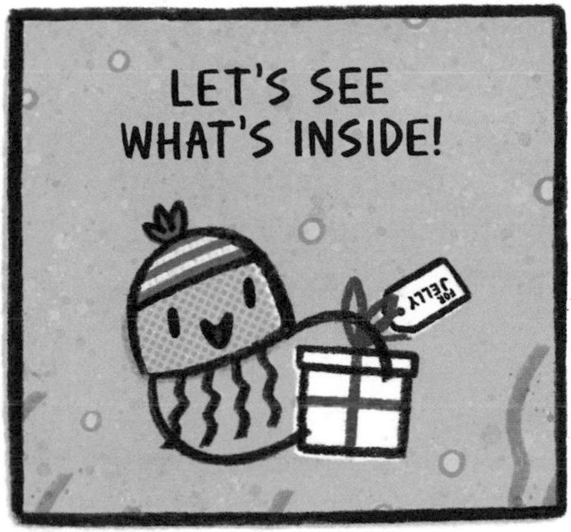
LET'S SEE WHAT'S INSIDE!
FOR JELLY

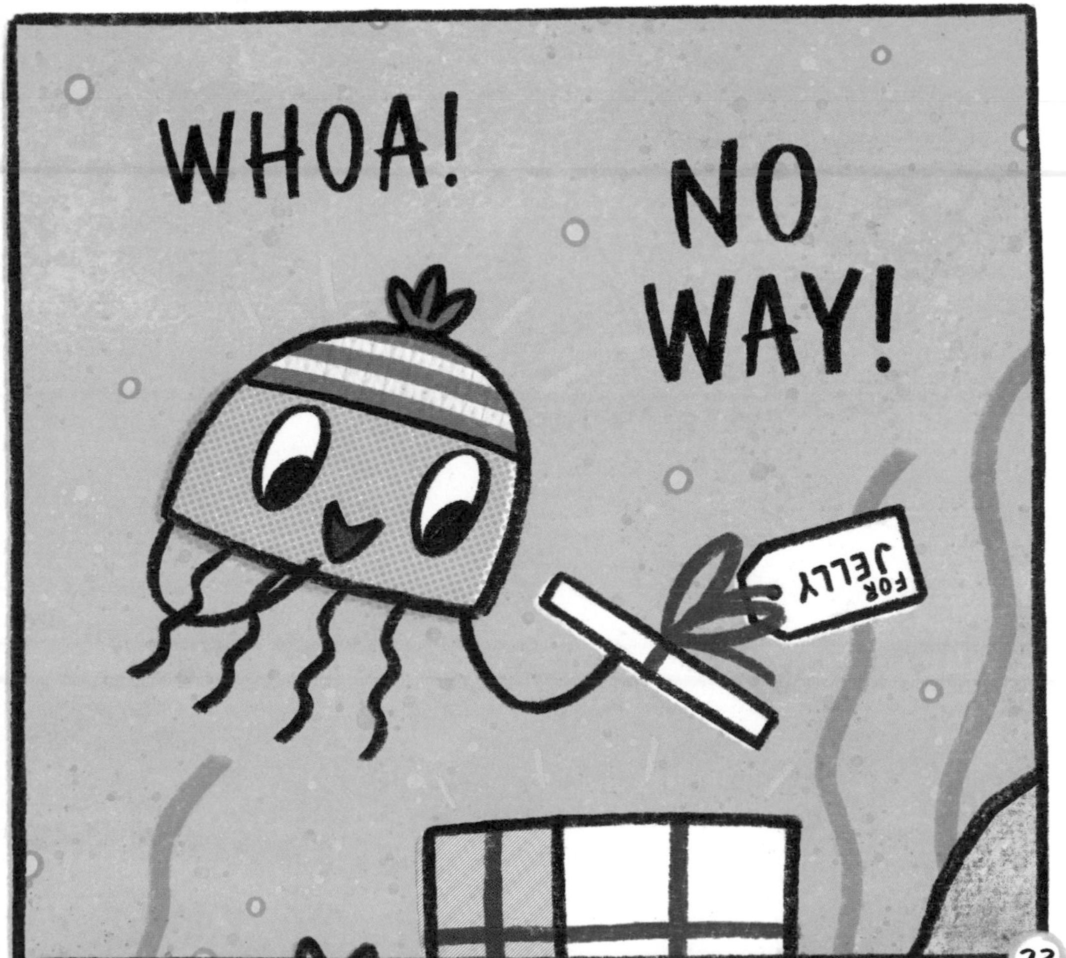
WHOA!
NO WAY!
FOR JELLY

MITTENS!

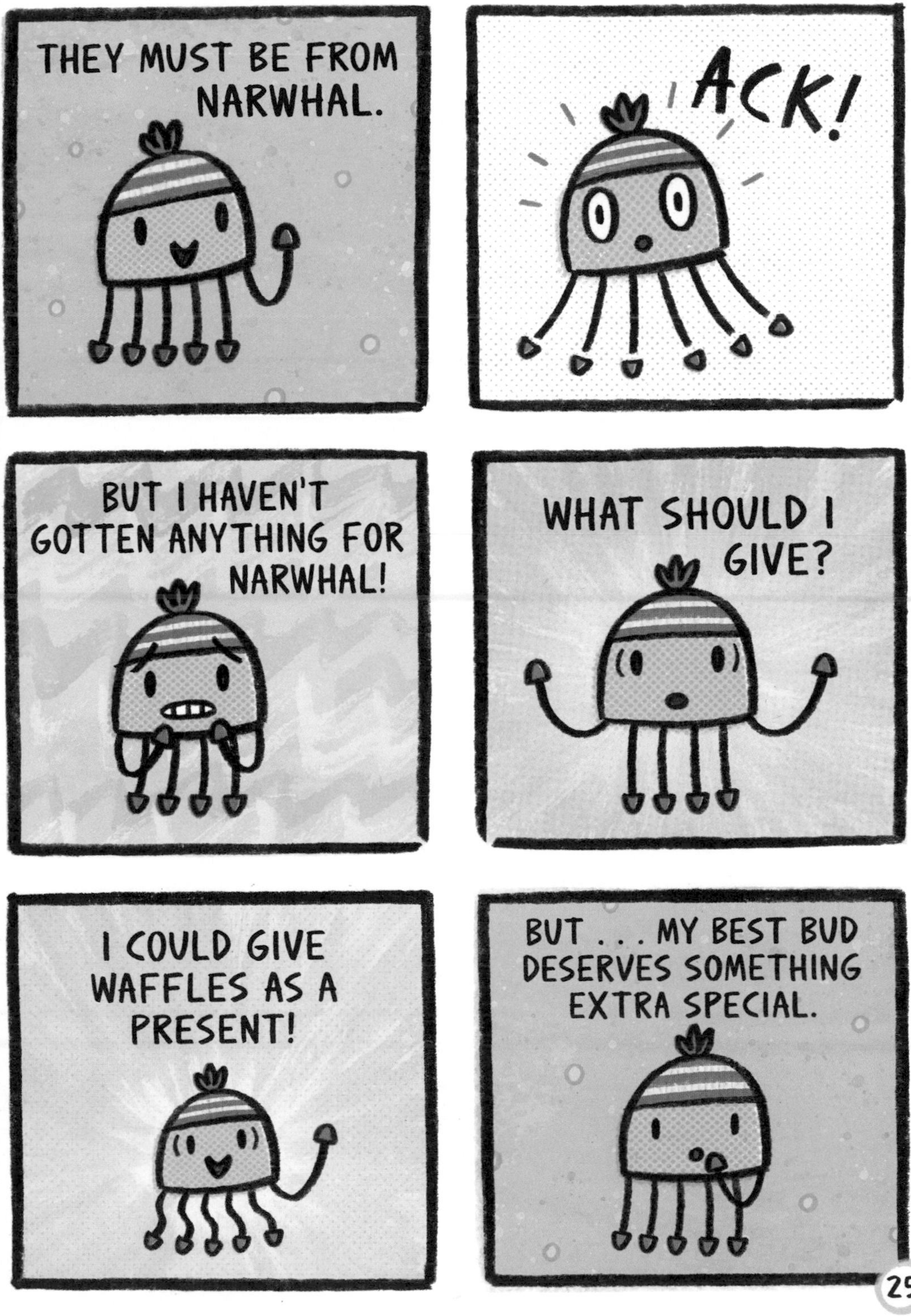
THEY MUST BE FROM NARWHAL.
ACK!
BUT I HAVEN'T GOTTEN ANYTHING FOR NARWHAL!
WHAT SHOULD I GIVE?
I COULD GIVE WAFFLES AS A PRESENT!
BUT . . . MY BEST BUD DESERVES SOMETHING EXTRA SPECIAL.

SOMETHING AS SUPER AND UNIQUE AS NARWHAL!

NARWHAL LIKES ROBOTS . . .

HAS ALWAYS WANTED WINGS . . .

AND LOVES
POLKA DOTS!

HOW ABOUT . . .

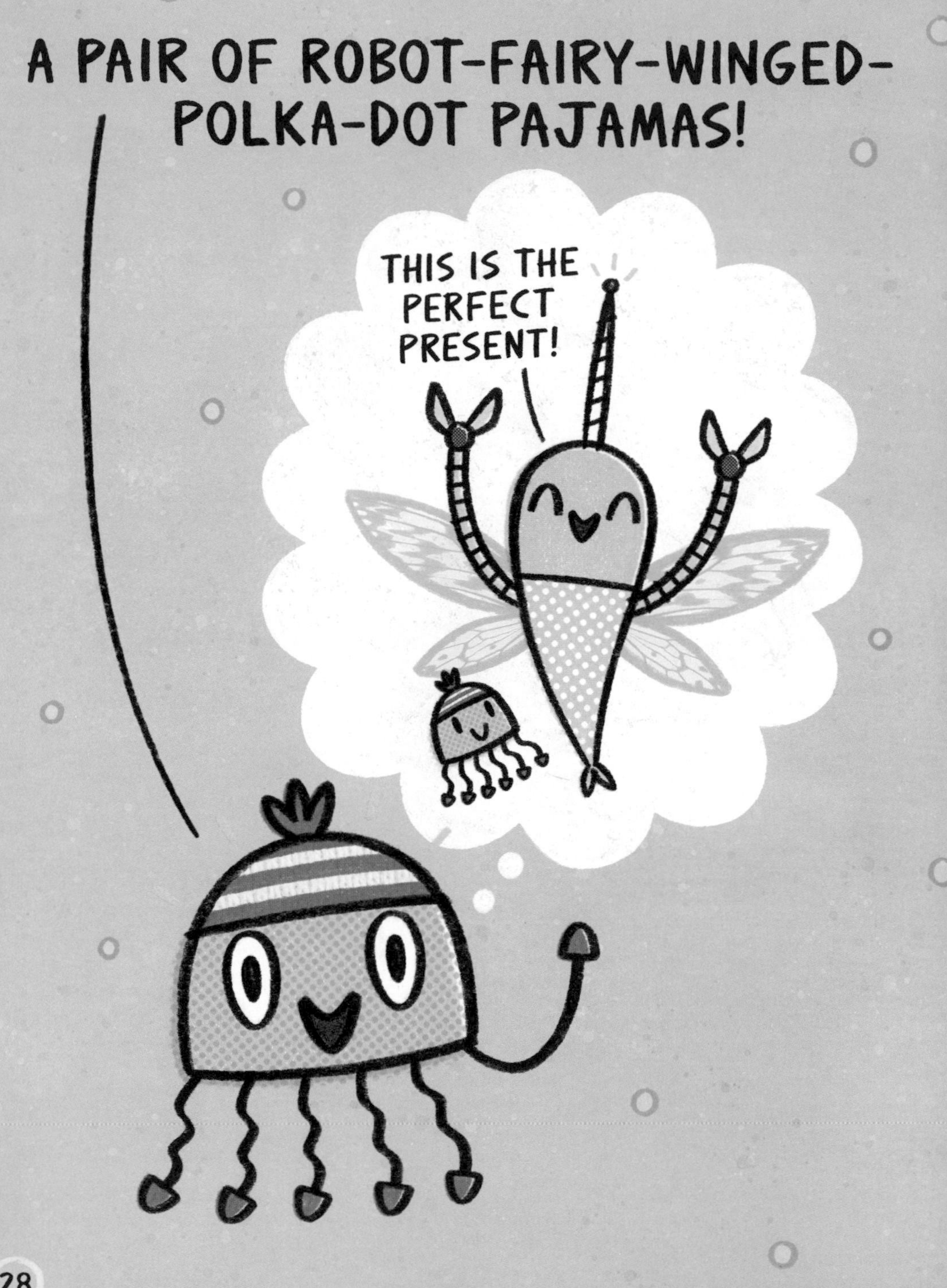
A PAIR OF ROBOT-FAIRY-WINGED-POLKA-DOT PAJAMAS!
THIS IS THE PERFECT PRESENT!

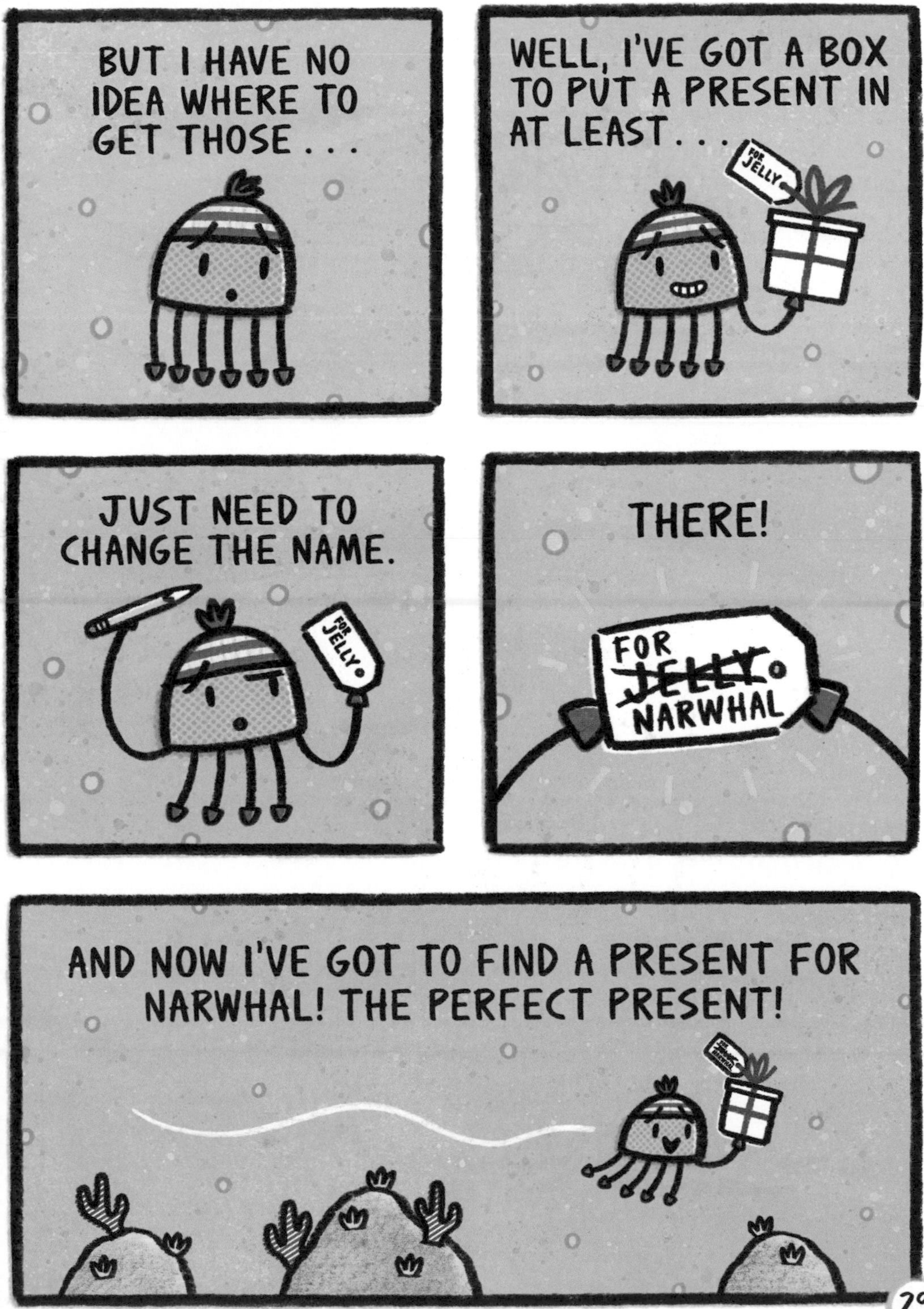
BUT I HAVE NO IDEA WHERE TO GET THOSE . . .
WELL, I'VE GOT A BOX TO PUT A PRESENT IN AT LEAST . . .
FOR JELLY
JUST NEED TO CHANGE THE NAME.
FOR JELLY
THERE!
FOR ~~JELLY~~ NARWHAL
AND NOW I'VE GOT TO FIND A PRESENT FOR NARWHAL! THE PERFECT PRESENT!

3 HOURS, 41 MINUTES AND 17 SECONDS LATER . . .

FINDING THE PERFECT PRESENT IS PRETTY TOUGH.

FOR ~~JELLY~~ NARWHAL

MAYBE I NEED SOME HELP . . .

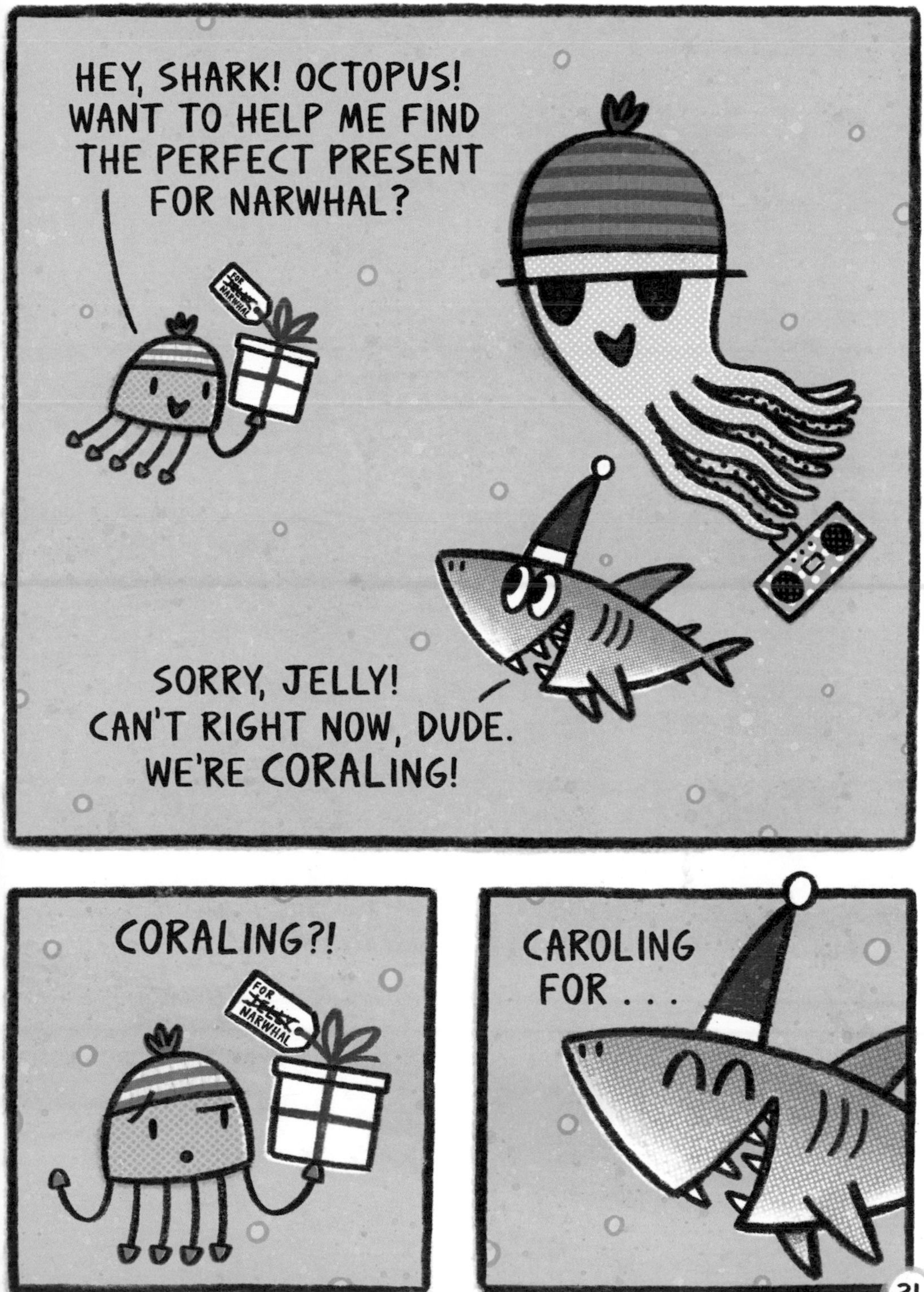
HEY, SHARK! OCTOPUS! WANT TO HELP ME FIND THE PERFECT PRESENT FOR NARWHAL?
FOR
NARWHAL
SORRY, JELLY! CAN'T RIGHT NOW, DUDE. WE'RE CORALING!
CORALING?!
FOR
NARWHAL
CAROLING FOR . . .

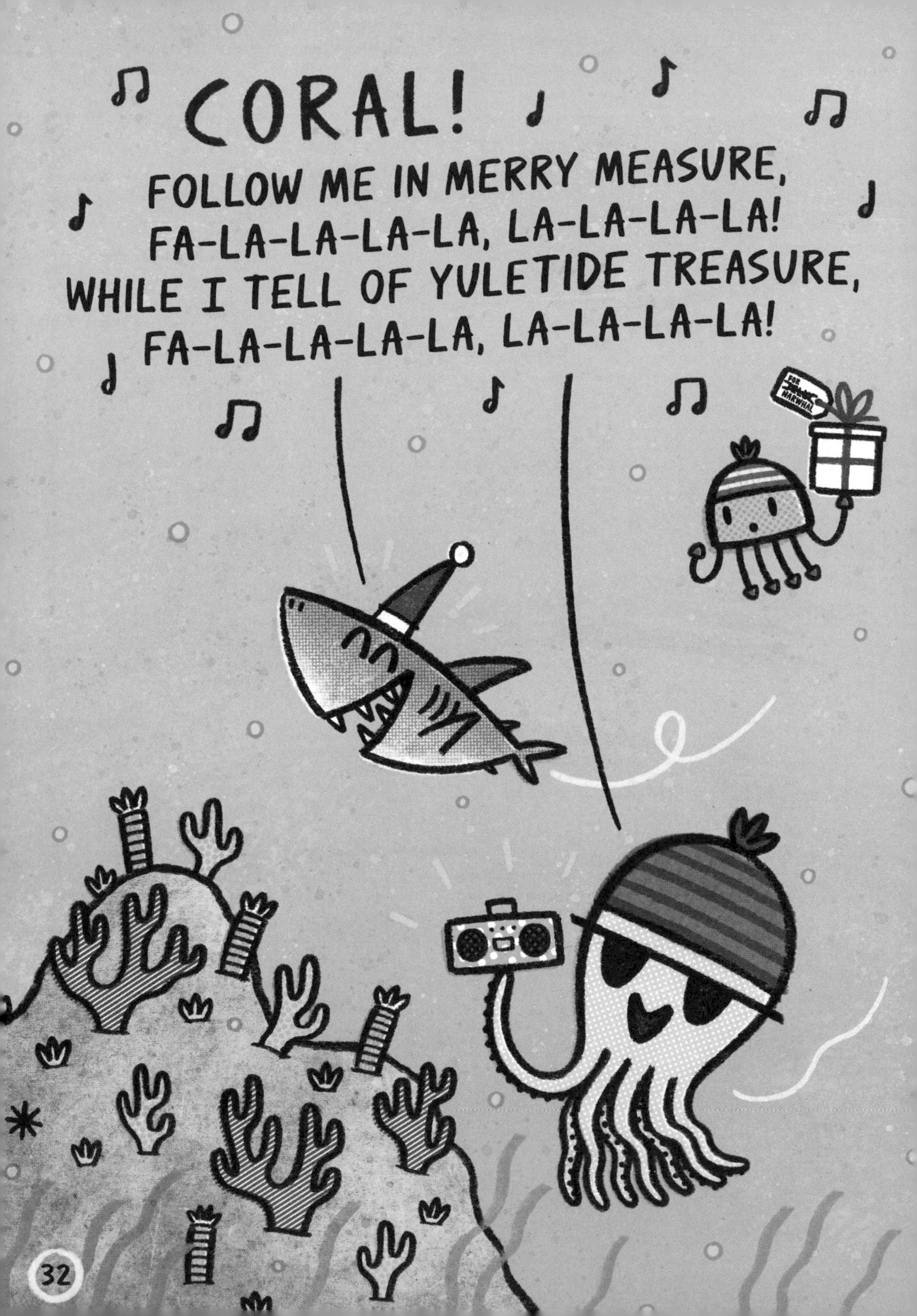
CORAL!
FOLLOW ME IN MERRY MEASURE,
FA-LA-LA-LA-LA, LA-LA-LA-LA!
WHILE I TELL OF YULETIDE TREASURE,
FA-LA-LA-LA-LA, LA-LA-LA-LA!

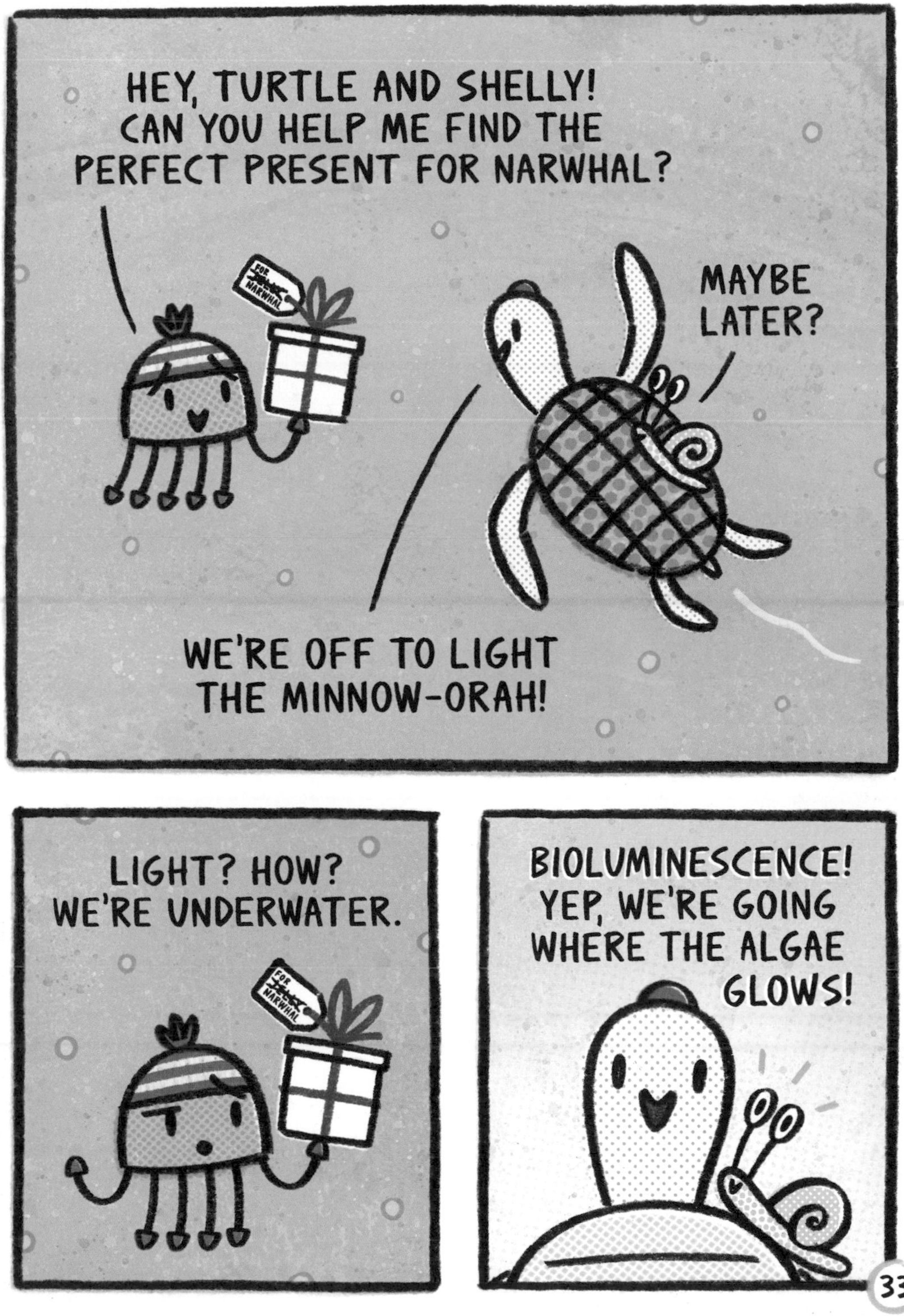
HEY, TURTLE AND SHELLY! CAN YOU HELP ME FIND THE PERFECT PRESENT FOR NARWHAL?
MAYBE LATER?
WE'RE OFF TO LIGHT THE MINNOW-ORAH!
LIGHT? HOW? WE'RE UNDERWATER.
BIOLUMINESCENCE! YEP, WE'RE GOING WHERE THE ALGAE GLOWS!

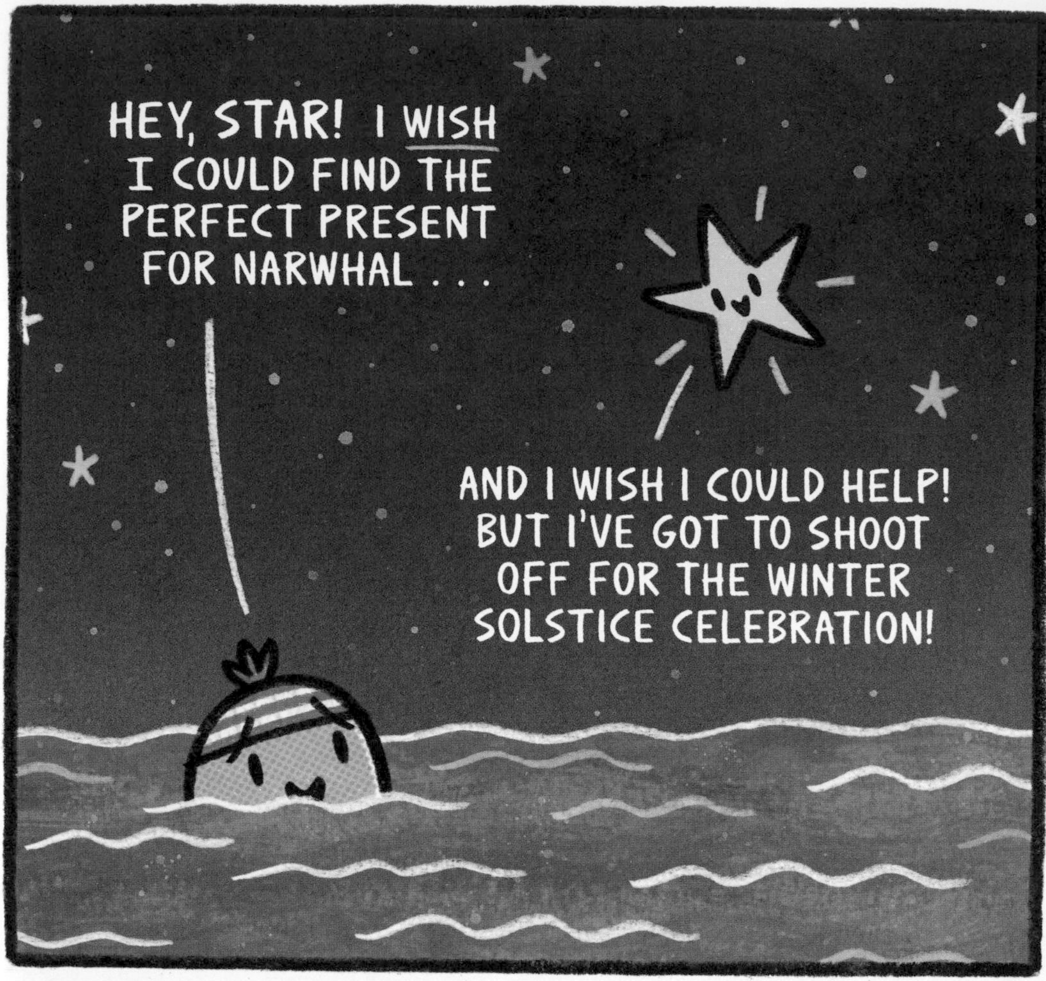
HEY, STAR! I WISH I COULD FIND THE PERFECT PRESENT FOR NARWHAL . . .
AND I WISH I COULD HELP! BUT I'VE GOT TO SHOOT OFF FOR THE WINTER SOLSTICE CELEBRATION!

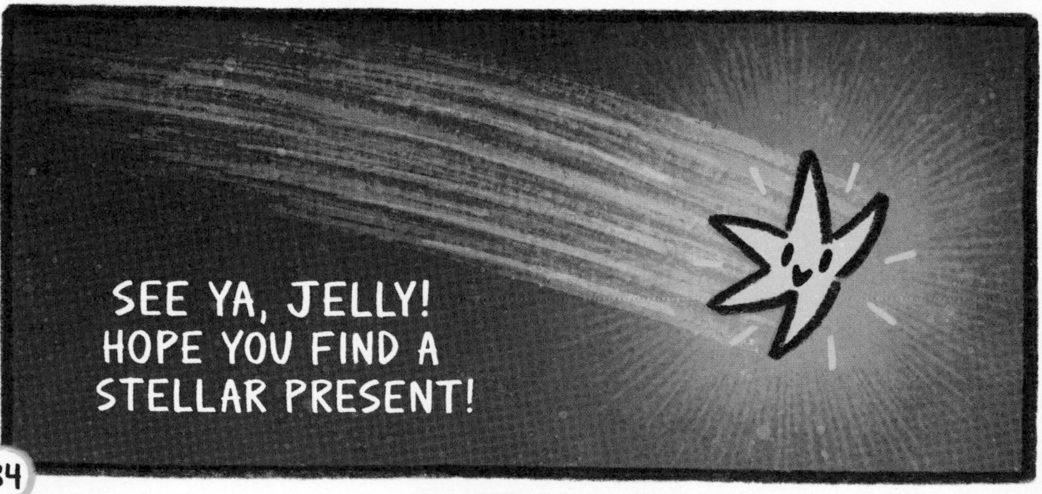
SEE YA, JELLY! HOPE YOU FIND A STELLAR PRESENT!

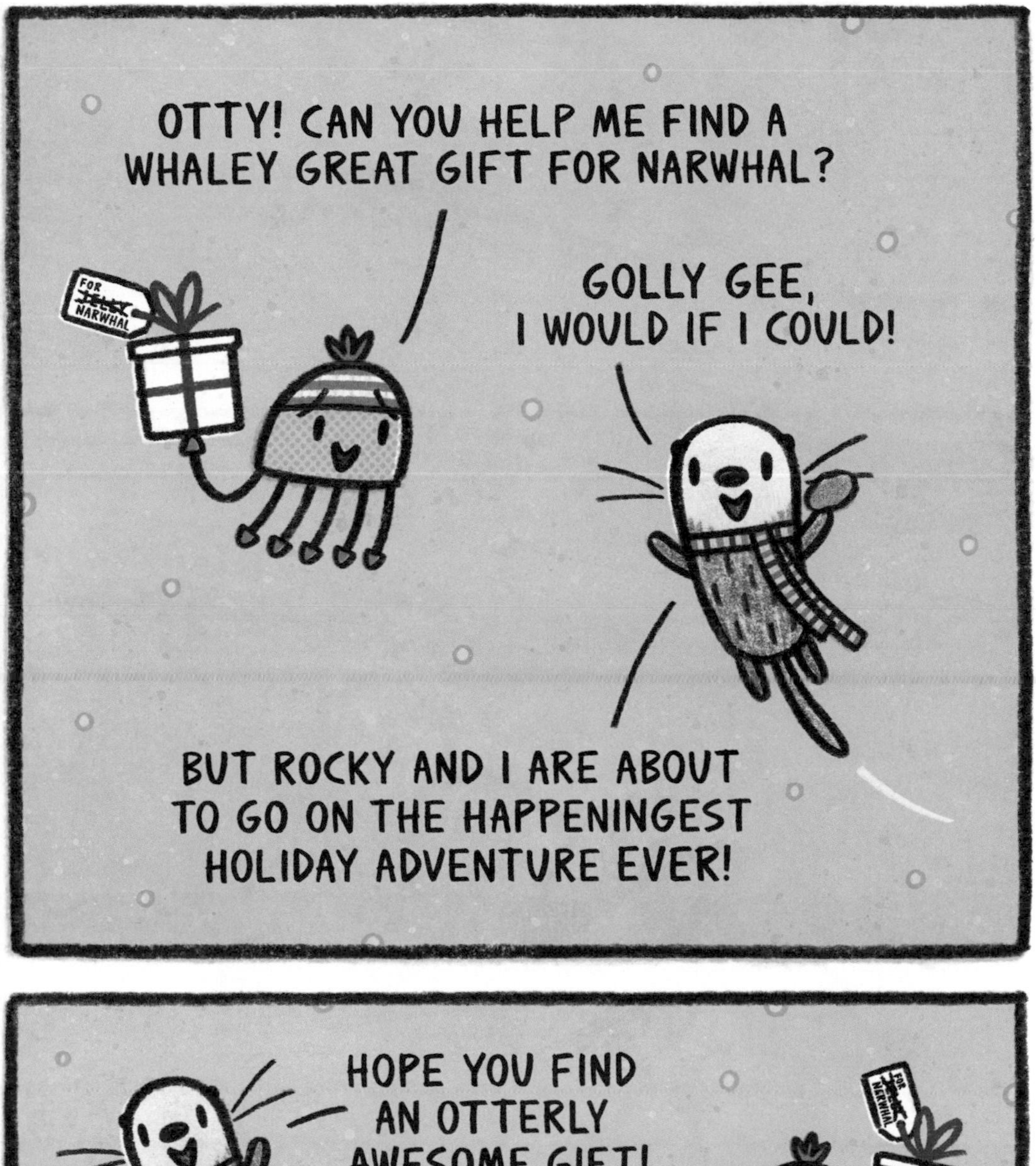
FOR NARWHAL
OTTY! CAN YOU HELP ME FIND A WHALEY GREAT GIFT FOR NARWHAL?
GOLLY GEE, I WOULD IF I COULD!
BUT ROCKY AND I ARE ABOUT TO GO ON THE HAPPENINGEST HOLIDAY ADVENTURE EVER!

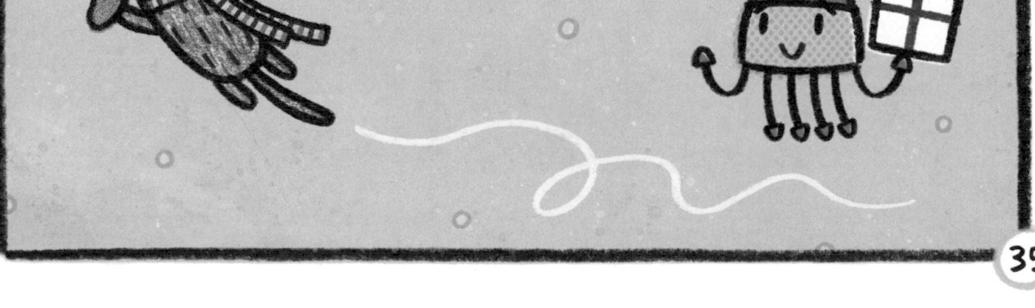
HOPE YOU FIND AN OTTERLY AWESOME GIFT!
FOR NARWHAL

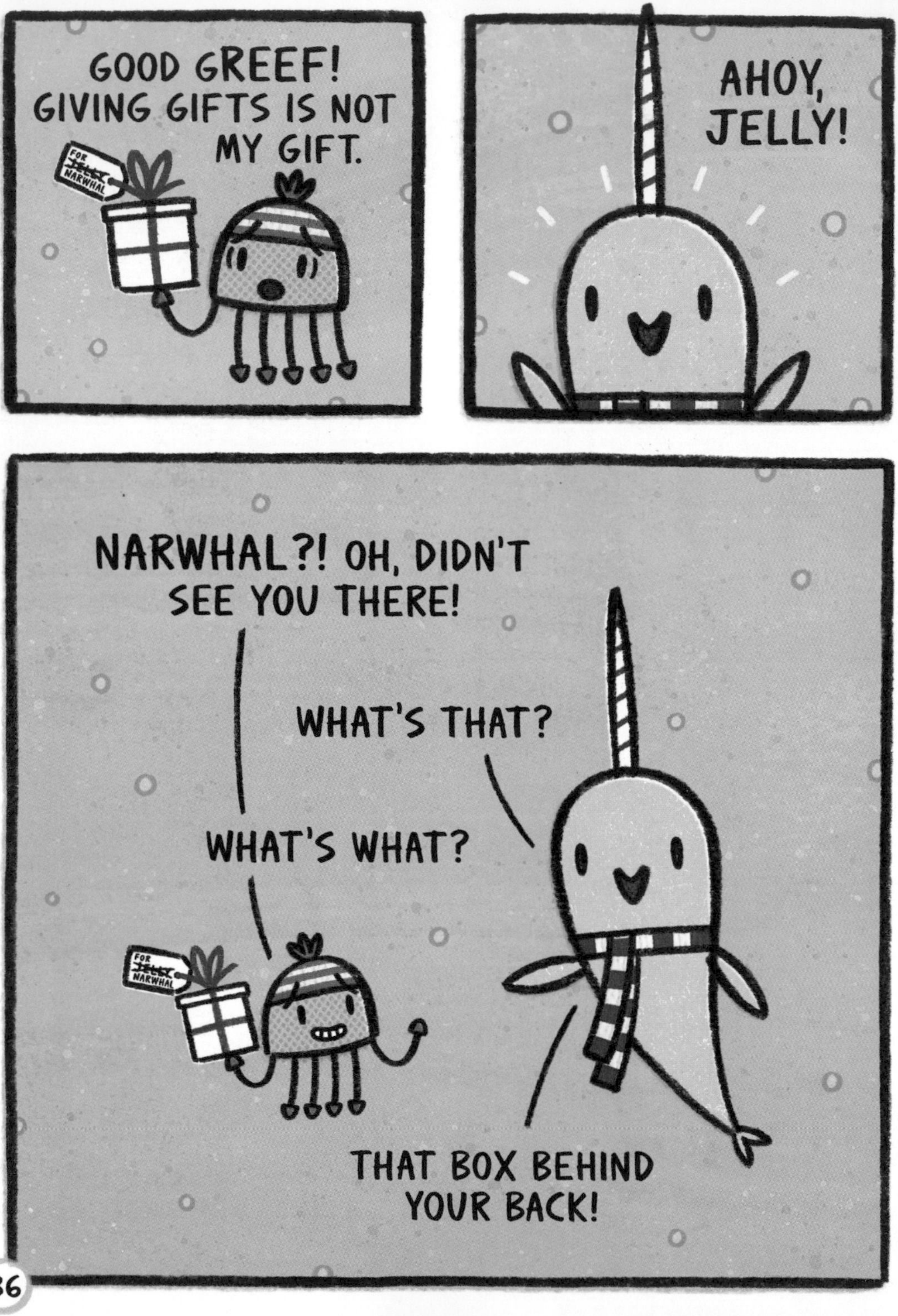
GOOD GREEF!
GIVING GIFTS IS NOT MY GIFT.
FOR JELLY NARWHAL
AHOY, JELLY!
NARWHAL?! OH, DIDN'T SEE YOU THERE!
WHAT'S THAT?
WHAT'S WHAT?
FOR JELLY NARWHAL
THAT BOX BEHIND YOUR BACK!

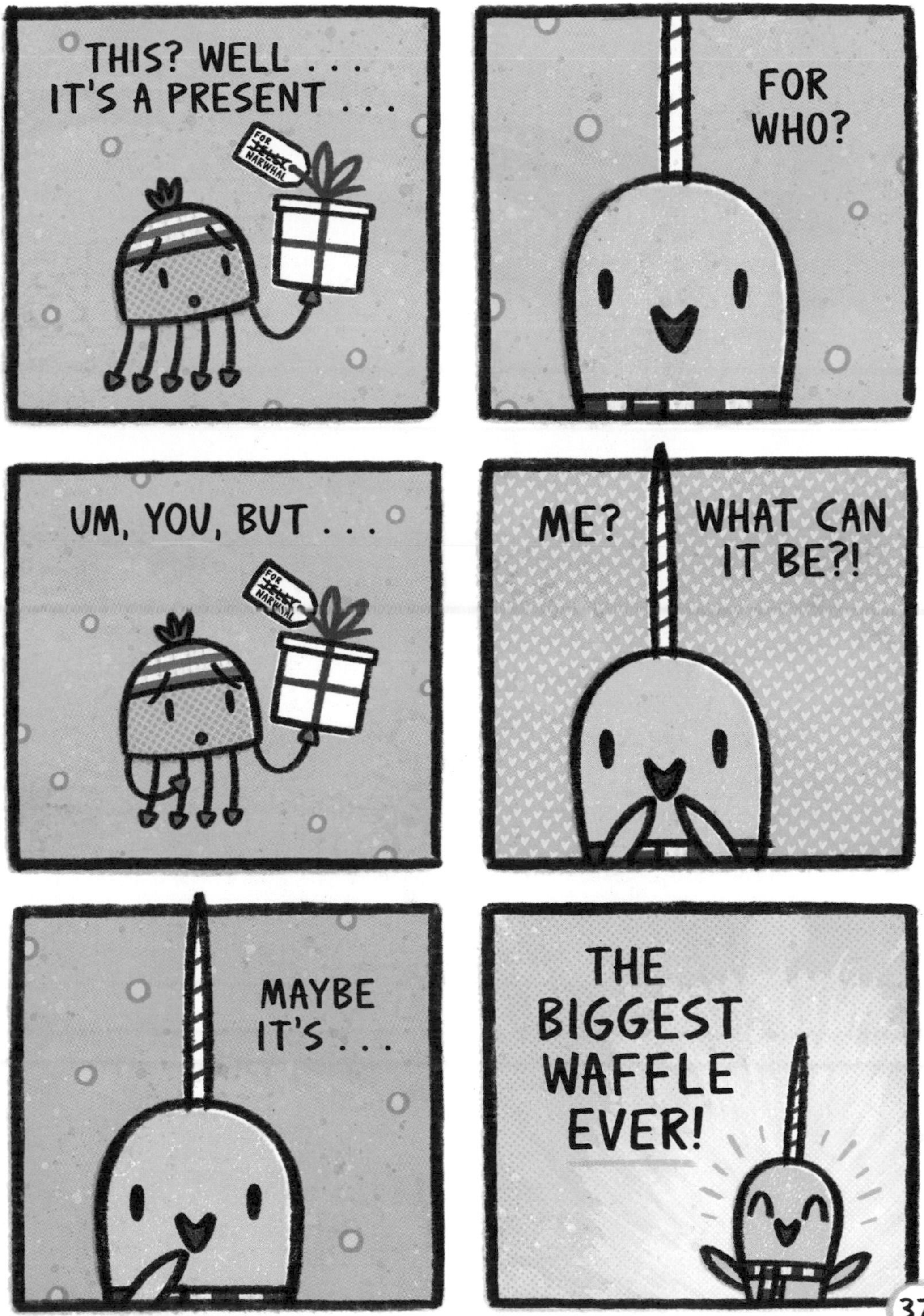
THIS? WELL . . . IT'S A PRESENT . . .
FOR WHO?
UM, YOU, BUT . . .
ME?
WHAT CAN IT BE?!
MAYBE IT'S . . .
THE BIGGEST WAFFLE EVER!

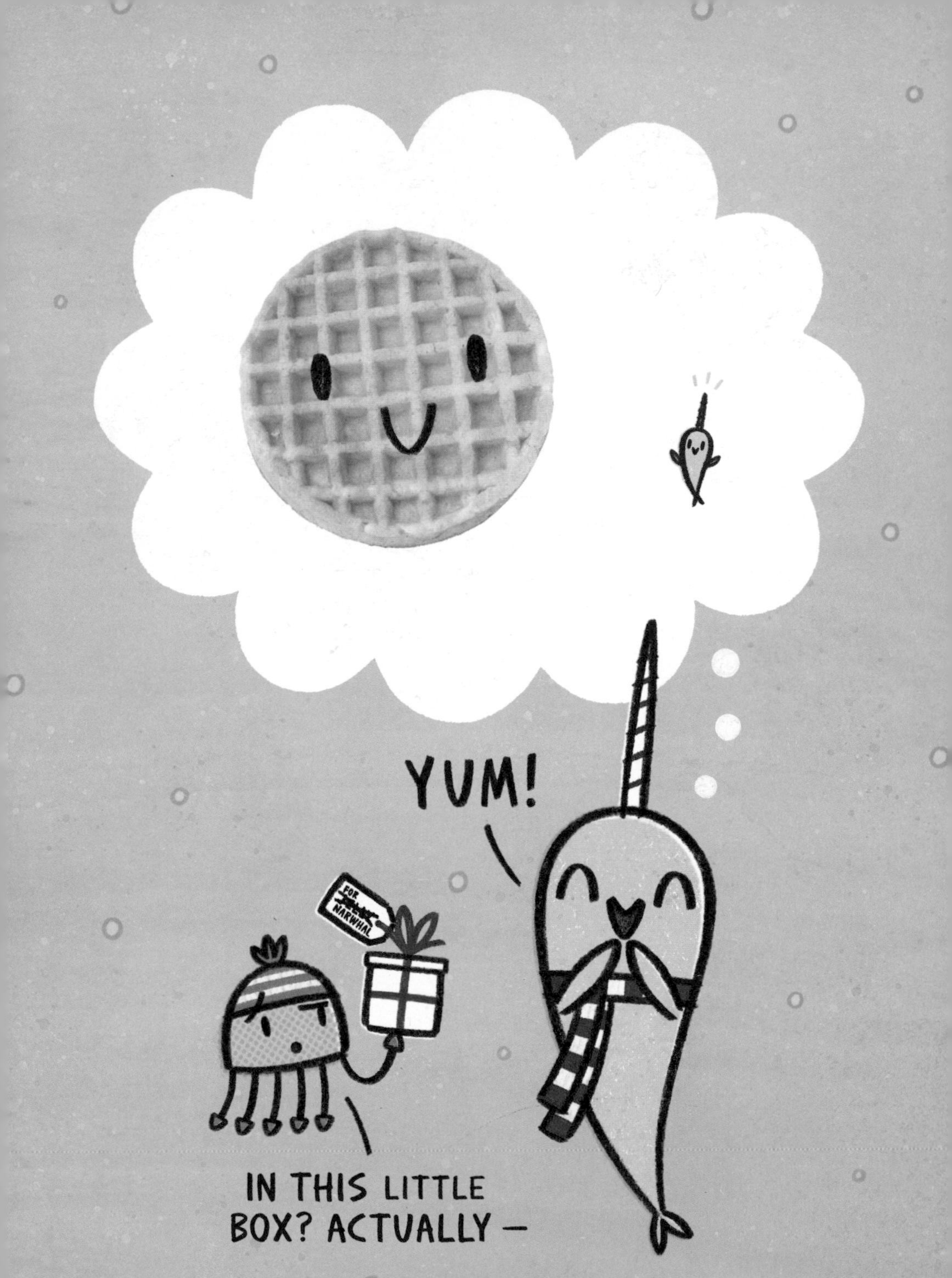
YUM!
FOR NARWHAL
IN THIS LITTLE BOX? ACTUALLY —

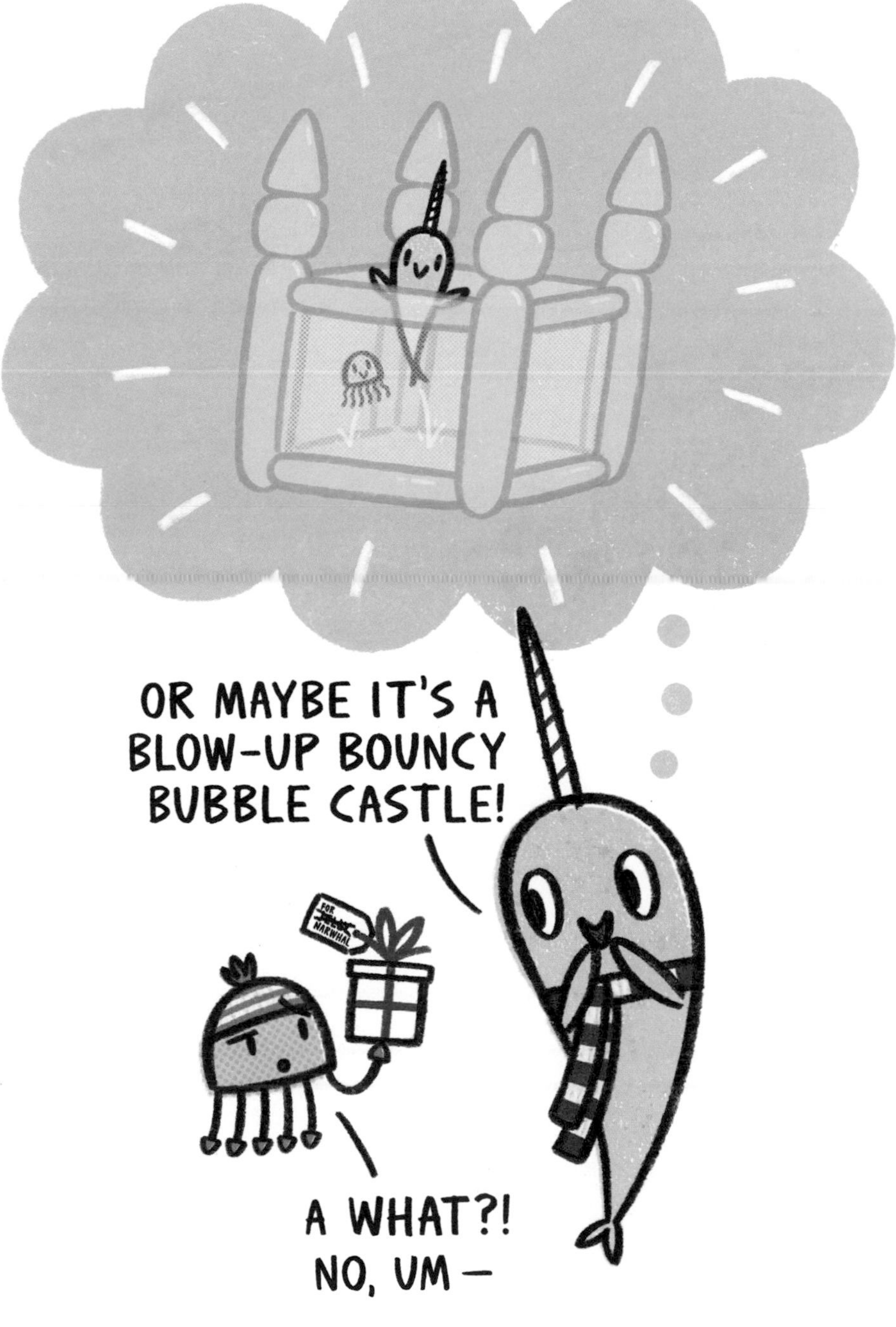
OR MAYBE IT'S A BLOW-UP BOUNCY BUBBLE CASTLE!
A WHAT?! NO, UM—

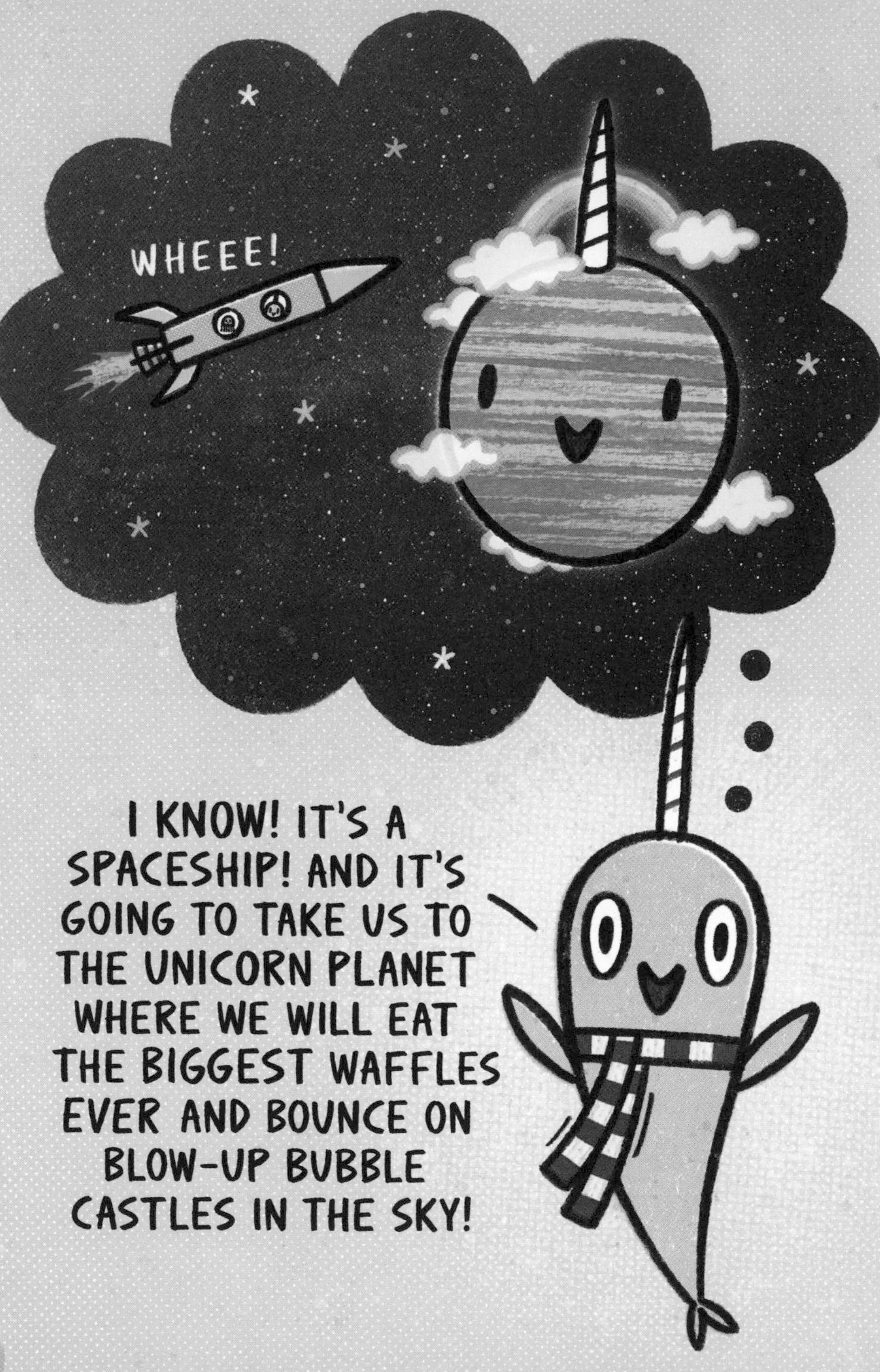
WHEEE!
I KNOW! IT'S A SPACESHIP! AND IT'S GOING TO TAKE US TO THE UNICORN PLANET WHERE WE WILL EAT THE BIGGEST WAFFLES EVER AND BOUNCE ON BLOW-UP BUBBLE CASTLES IN THE SKY!

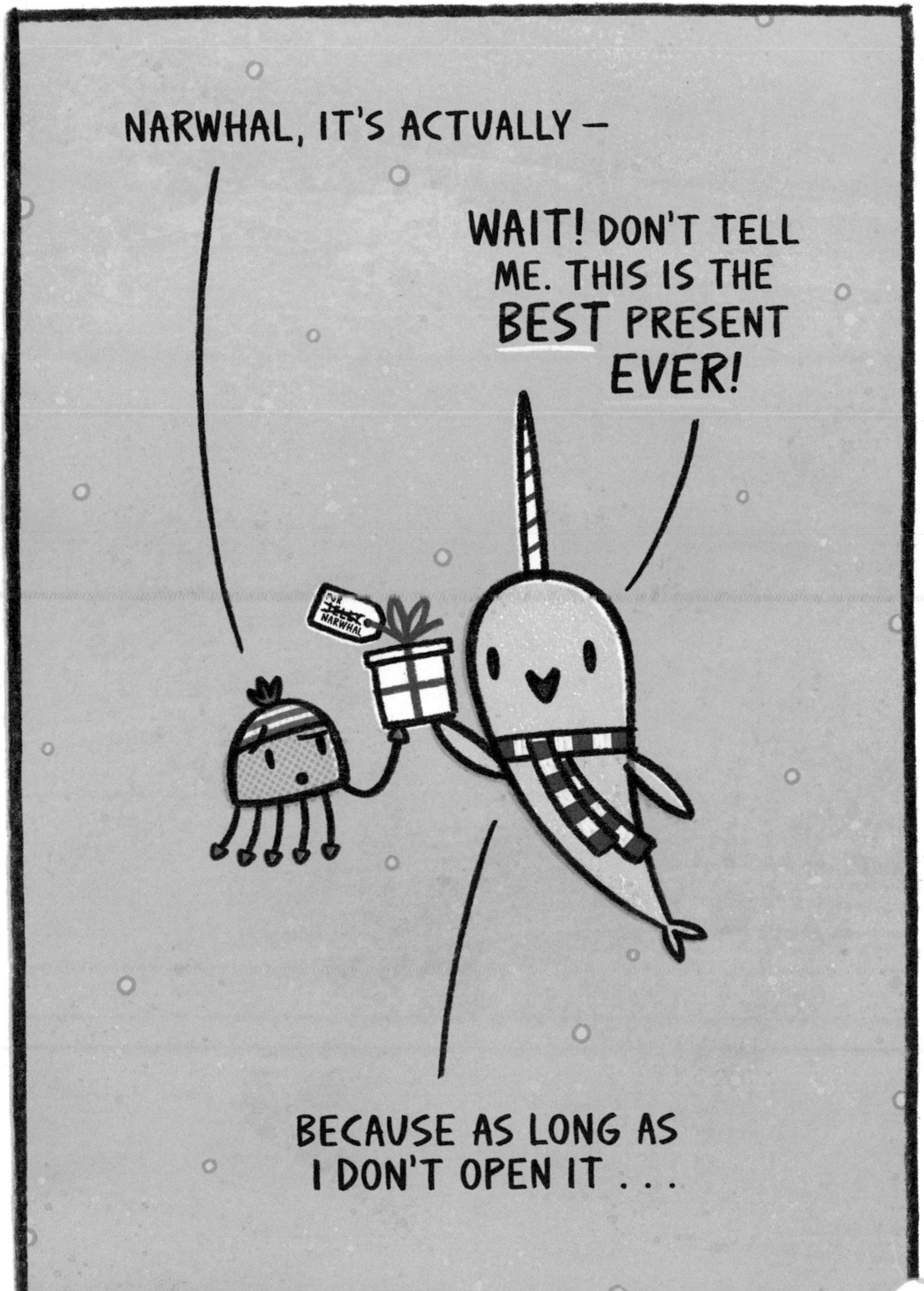
NARWHAL, IT'S ACTUALLY —
WAIT! DON'T TELL ME. THIS IS THE BEST PRESENT EVER!
BECAUSE AS LONG AS I DON'T OPEN IT . . .

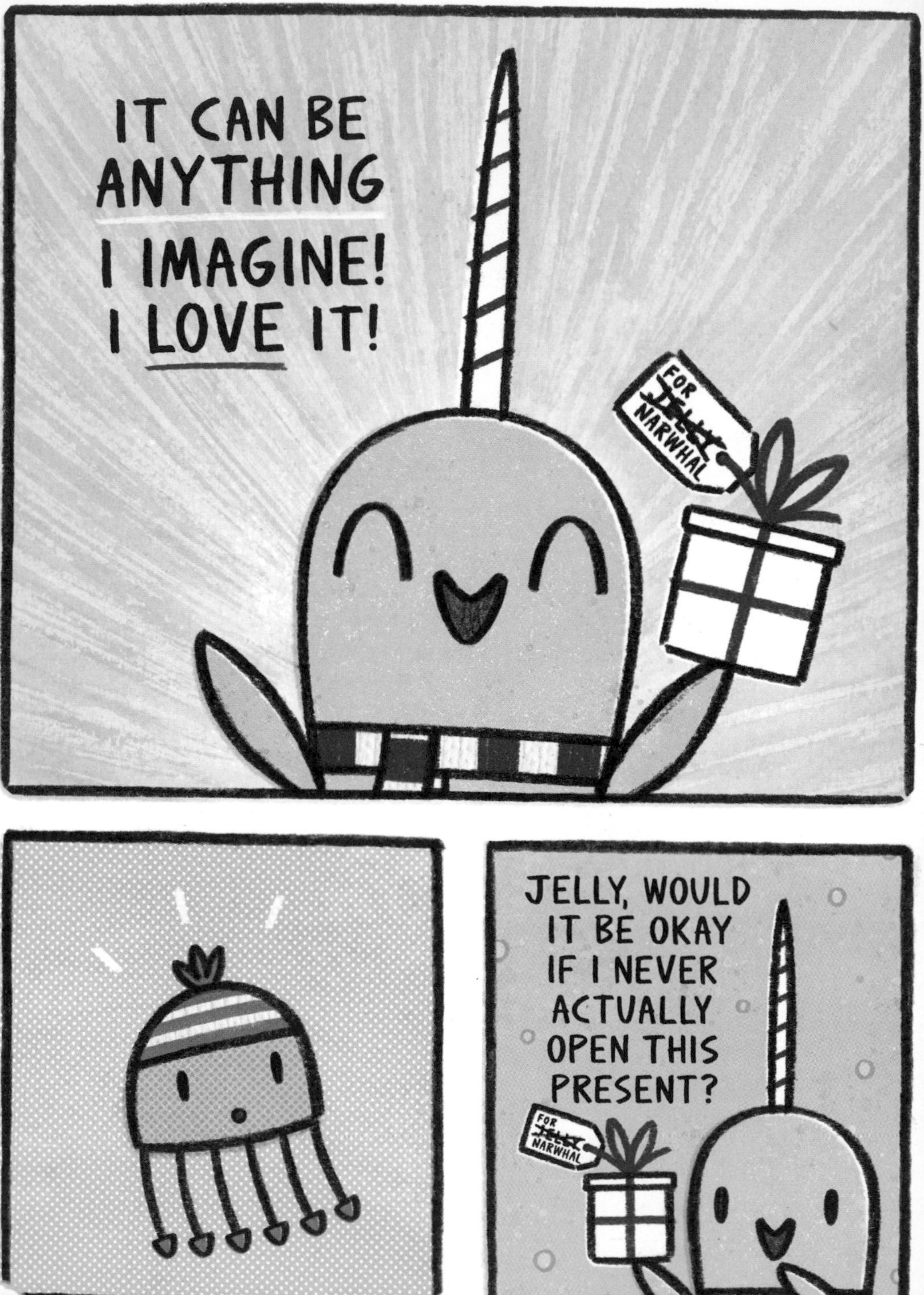
IT CAN BE ANYTHING I IMAGINE! I LOVE IT!
FOR ~~JELLY~~ NARWHAL
JELLY, WOULD IT BE OKAY IF I NEVER ACTUALLY OPEN THIS PRESENT?
FOR ~~JELLY~~ NARWHAL

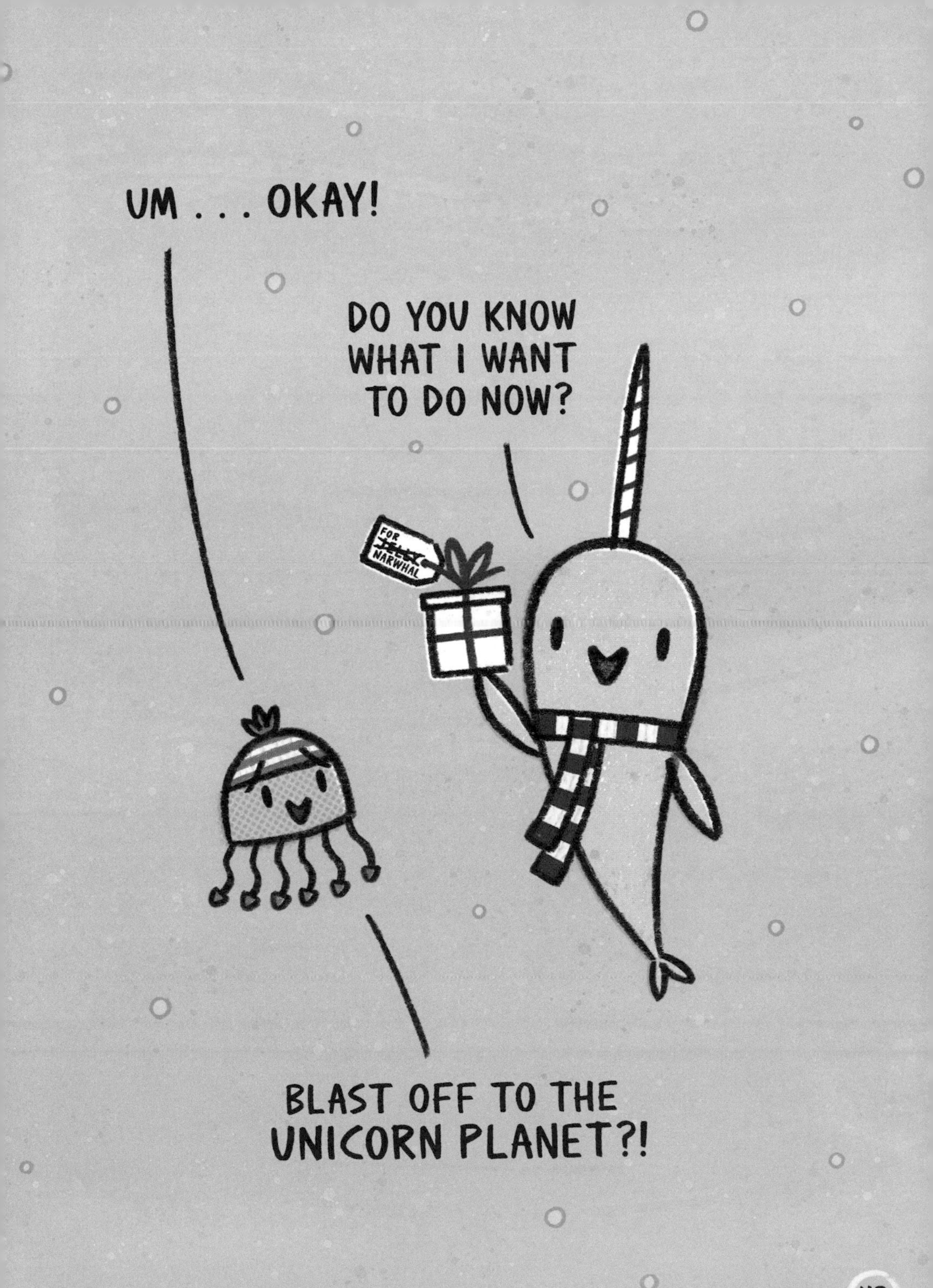
UM . . . OKAY!
DO YOU KNOW WHAT I WANT TO DO NOW?
FOR NARWHAL
BLAST OFF TO THE UNICORN PLANET?!

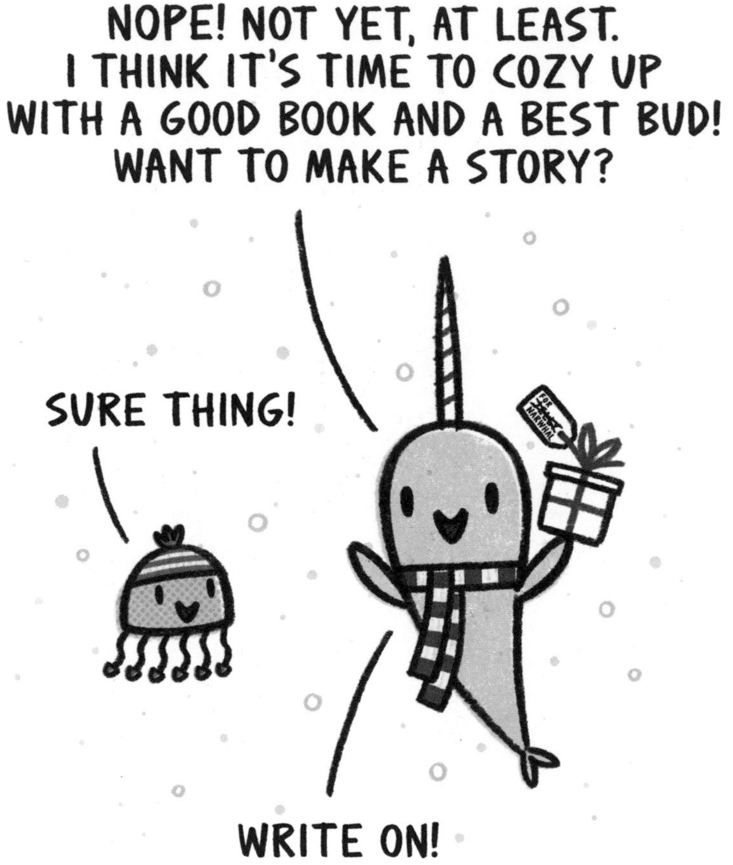
NOPE! NOT YET, AT LEAST. I THINK IT'S TIME TO COZY UP WITH A GOOD BOOK AND A BEST BUD! WANT TO MAKE A STORY?
SURE THING!
WRITE ON!

THE MEAN GREEN JELLY BEAN

by Narwhal and Jelly

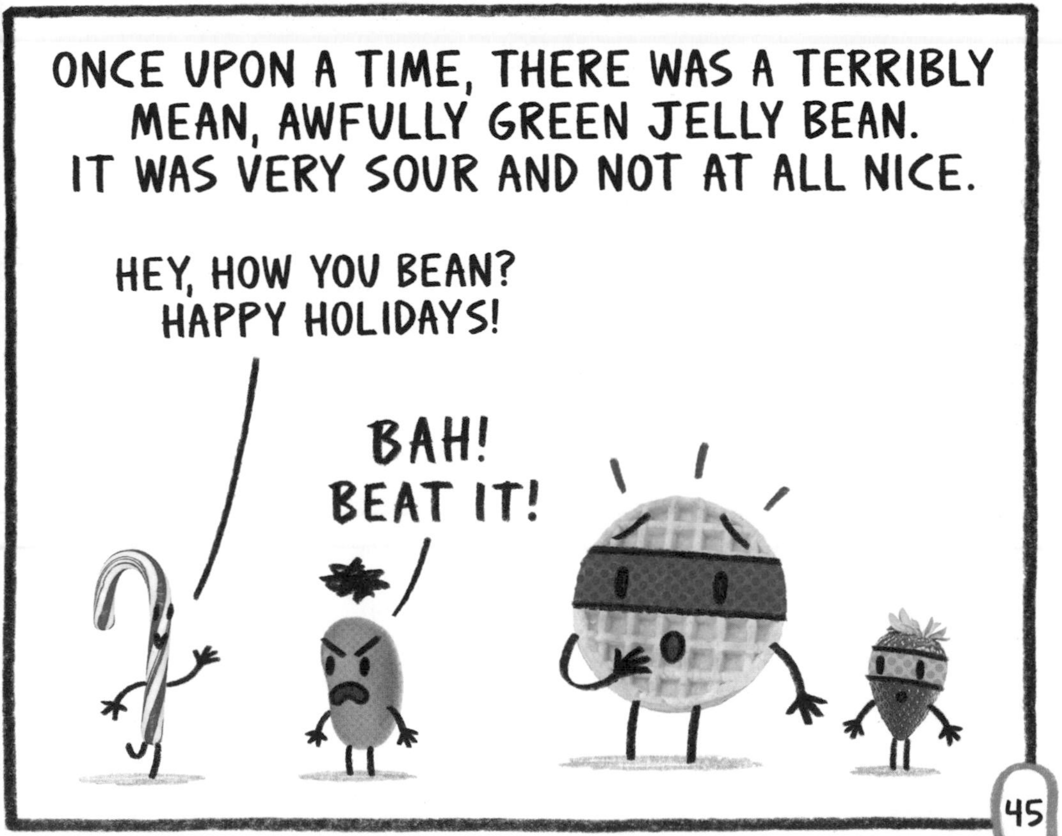
ONCE UPON A TIME, THERE WAS A TERRIBLY MEAN, AWFULLY GREEN JELLY BEAN. IT WAS VERY SOUR AND NOT AT ALL NICE.
HEY, HOW YOU BEAN? HAPPY HOLIDAYS!
BAH! BEAT IT!

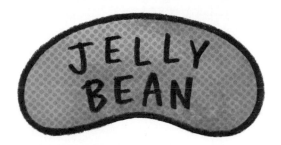

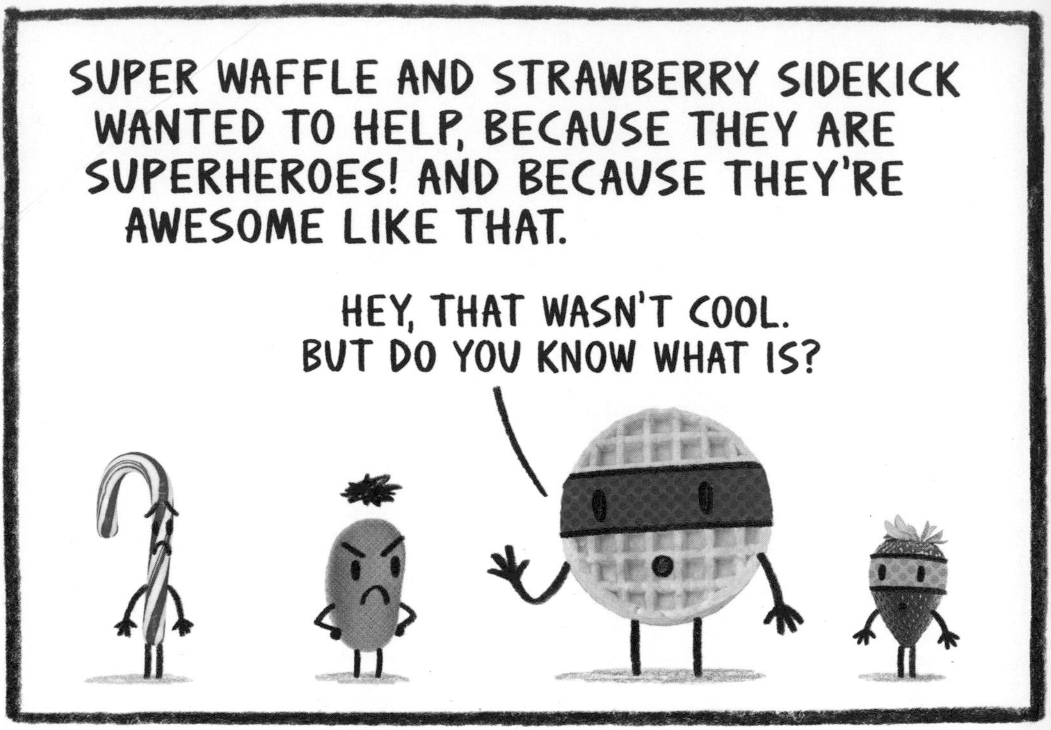
SUPER WAFFLE AND STRAWBERRY SIDEKICK WANTED TO HELP, BECAUSE THEY ARE SUPERHEROES! AND BECAUSE THEY'RE AWESOME LIKE THAT.
HEY, THAT WASN'T COOL. BUT DO YOU KNOW WHAT IS?

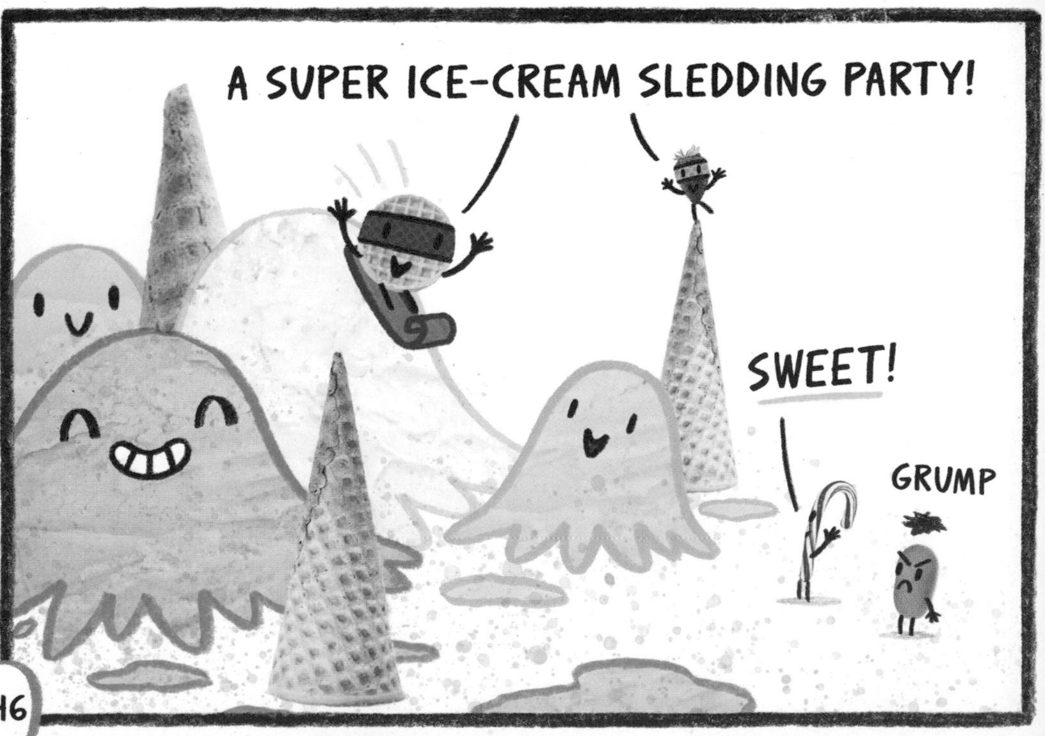
A SUPER ICE-CREAM SLEDDING PARTY!
SWEET!
GRUMP

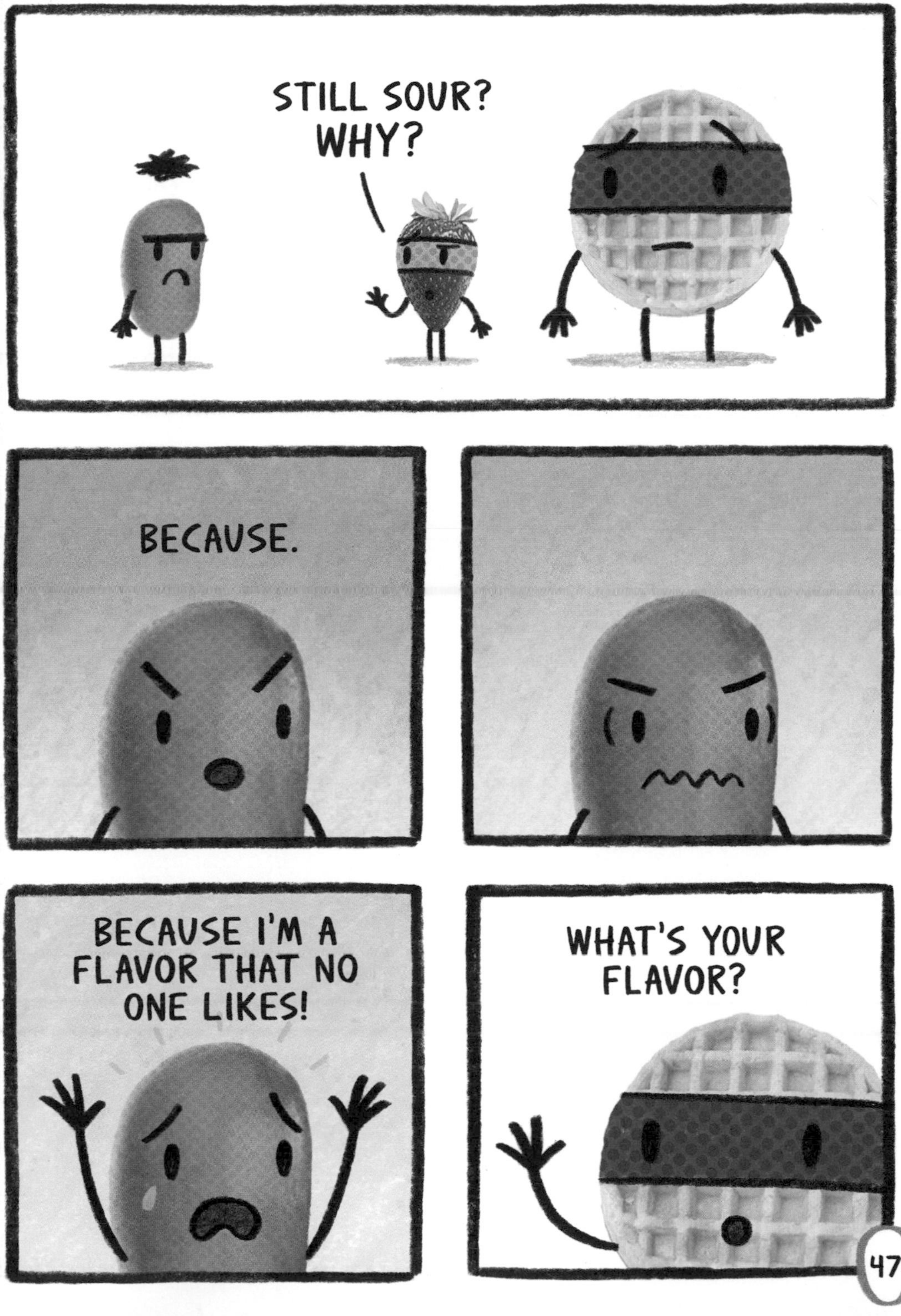
STILL SOUR?
WHY?
BECAUSE.
BECAUSE I'M A FLAVOR THAT NO ONE LIKES!
WHAT'S YOUR FLAVOR?

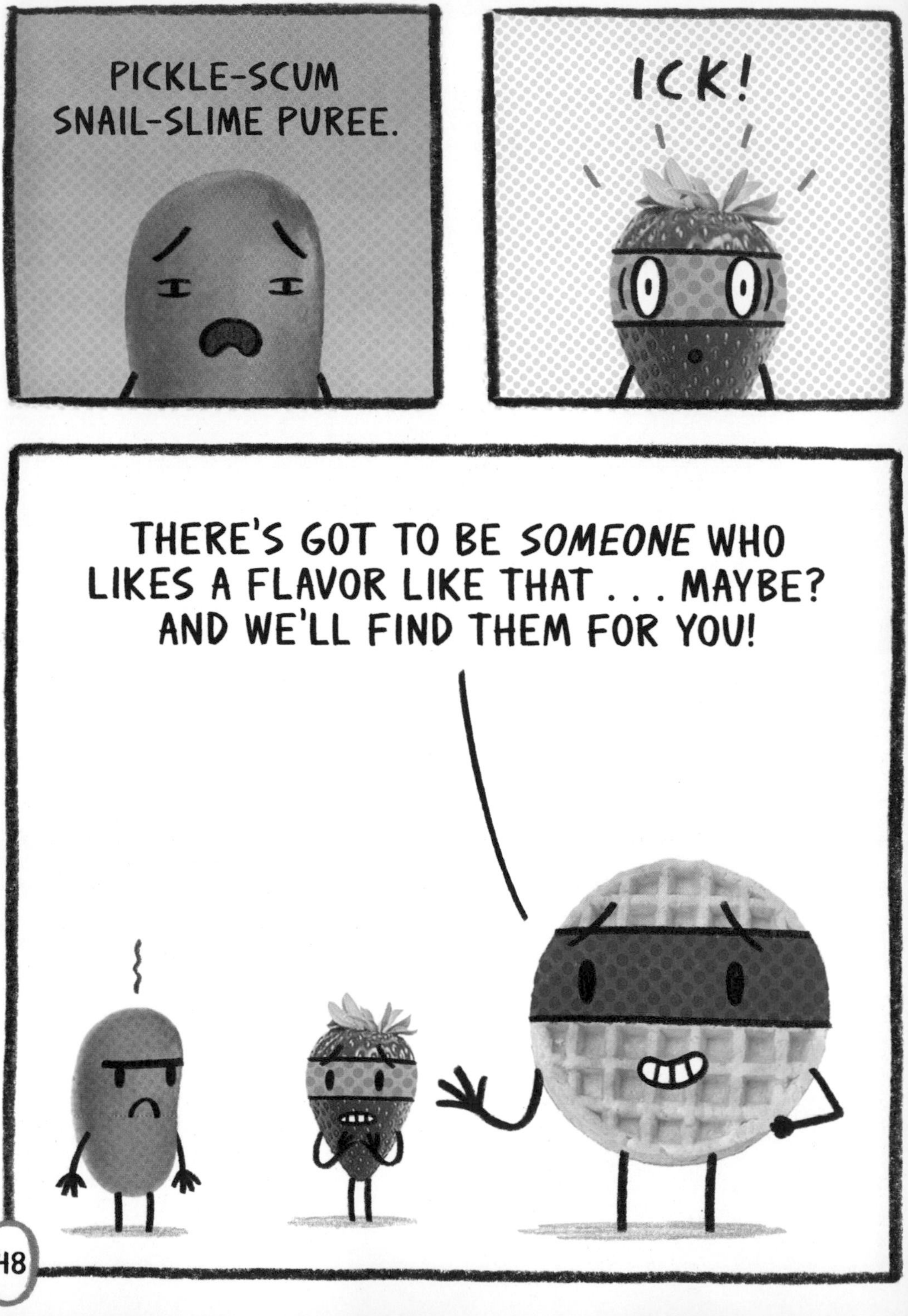
PICKLE-SCUM SNAIL-SLIME PUREE.
ICK!
THERE'S GOT TO BE *SOMEONE* WHO LIKES A FLAVOR LIKE THAT . . . MAYBE? AND WE'LL FIND THEM FOR YOU!

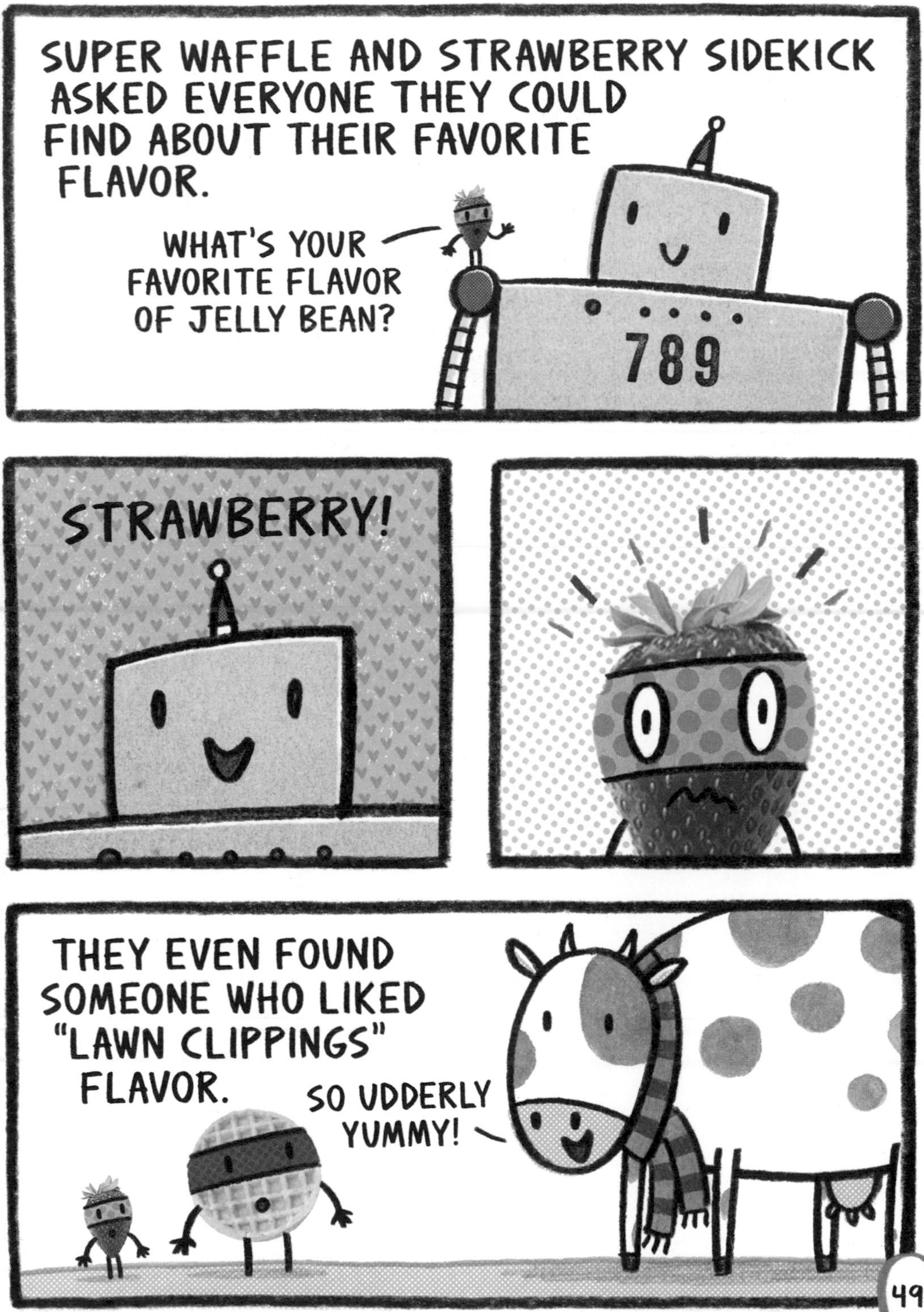

SUPER WAFFLE AND STRAWBERRY SIDEKICK ASKED EVERYONE THEY COULD FIND ABOUT THEIR FAVORITE FLAVOR.
WHAT'S YOUR FAVORITE FLAVOR OF JELLY BEAN?
789
STRAWBERRY!
THEY EVEN FOUND SOMEONE WHO LIKED "LAWN CLIPPINGS" FLAVOR.
SO UDDERLY YUMMY!

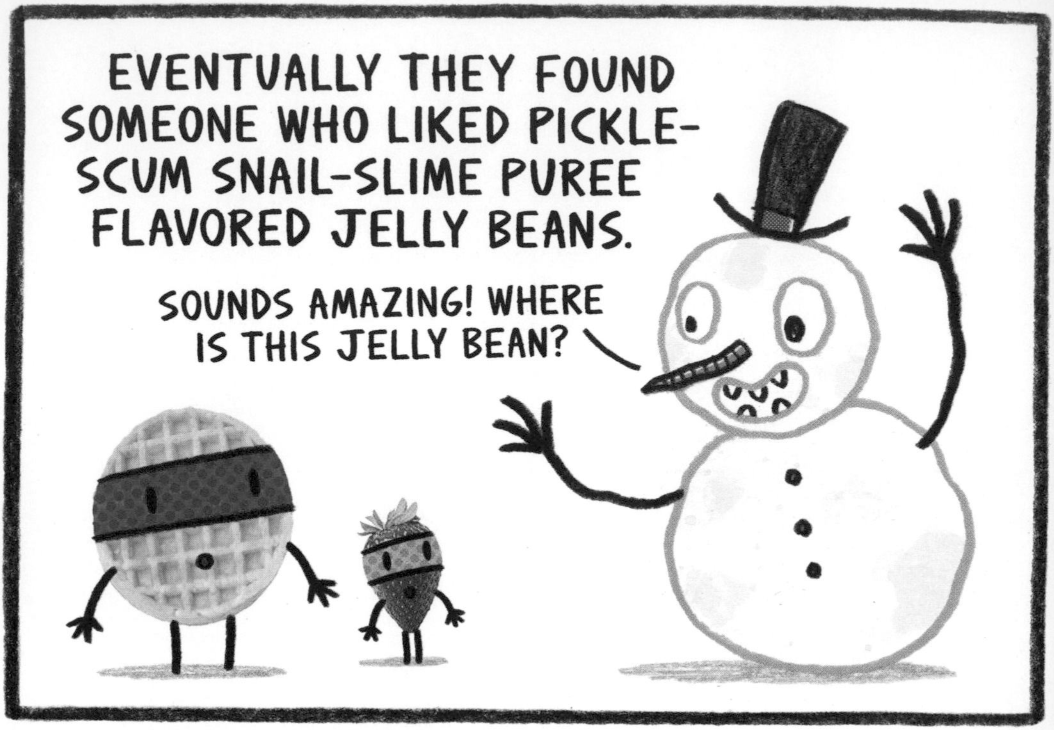
EVENTUALLY THEY FOUND SOMEONE WHO LIKED PICKLE-SCUM SNAIL-SLIME PUREE FLAVORED JELLY BEANS.
SOUNDS AMAZING! WHERE IS THIS JELLY BEAN?

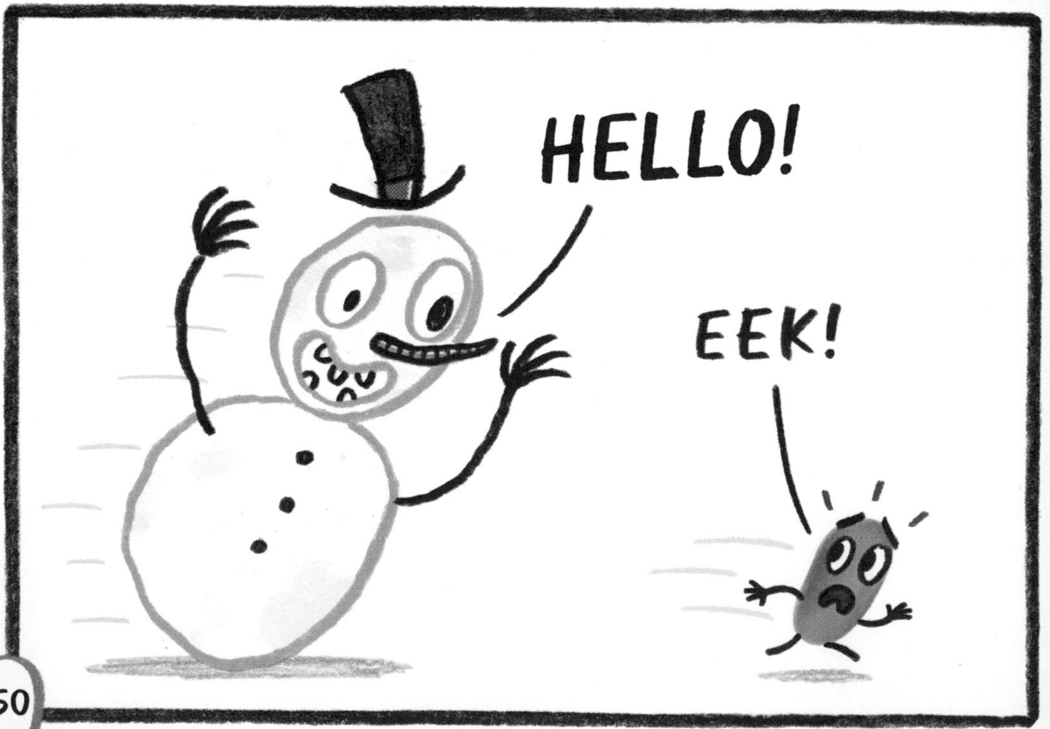
HELLO!
EEK!

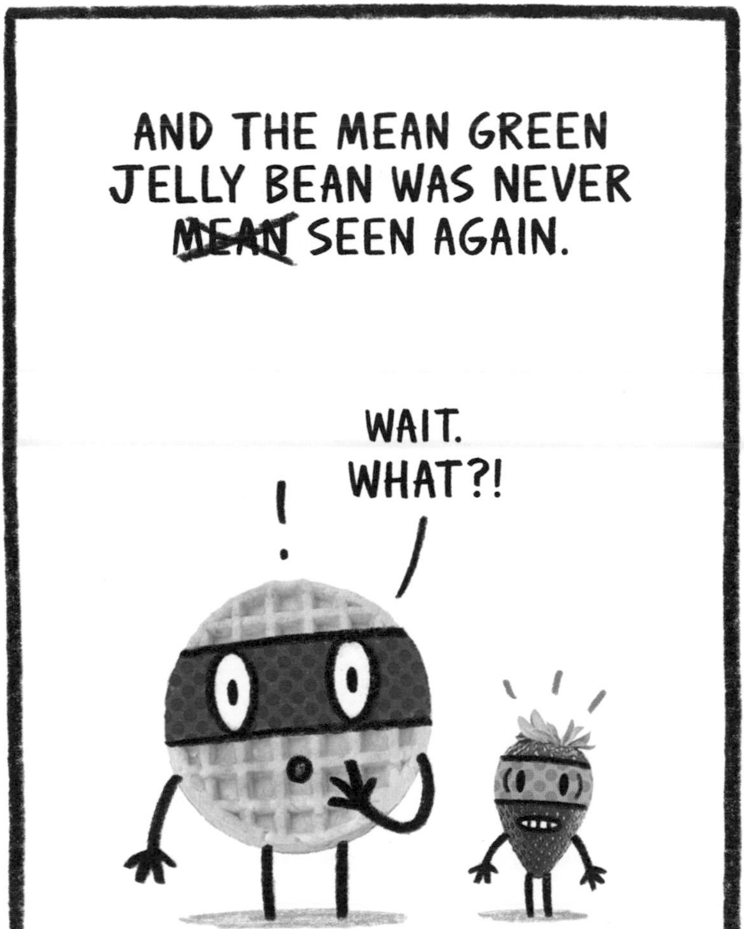
AND THE MEAN GREEN JELLY BEAN WAS NEVER ~~MEAN~~ SEEN AGAIN.
!
WAIT. WHAT?!

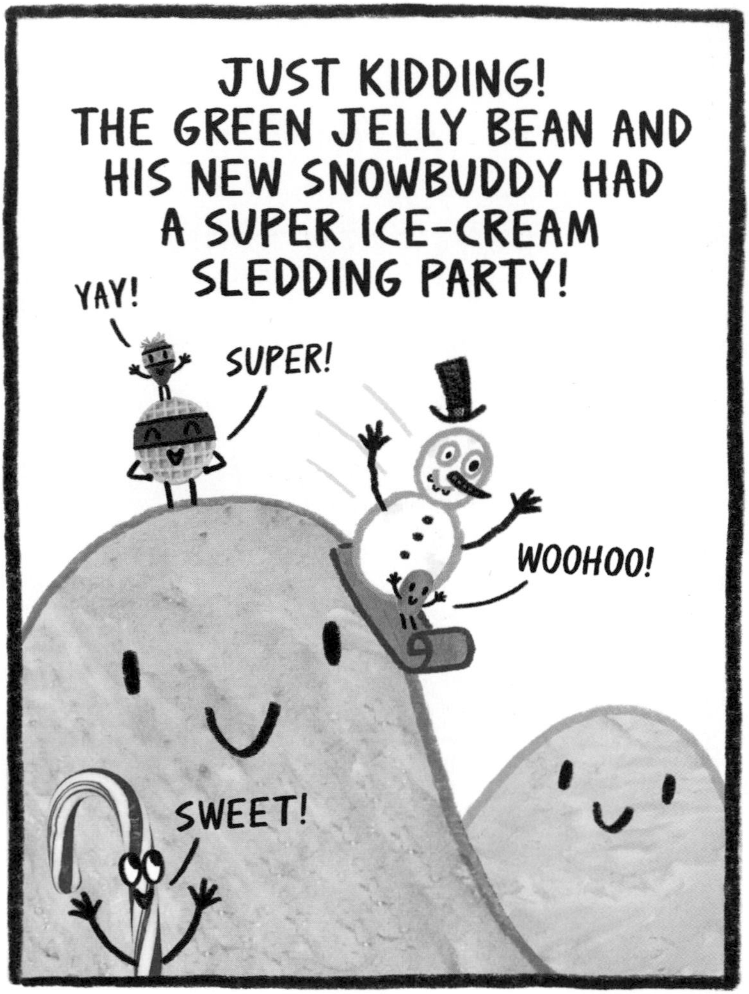
JUST KIDDING!
THE GREEN JELLY BEAN AND HIS NEW SNOWBUDDY HAD A SUPER ICE-CREAM SLEDDING PARTY!
YAY!
SUPER!
WOOHOO!
SWEET!

THE MERRY MERMICORN!

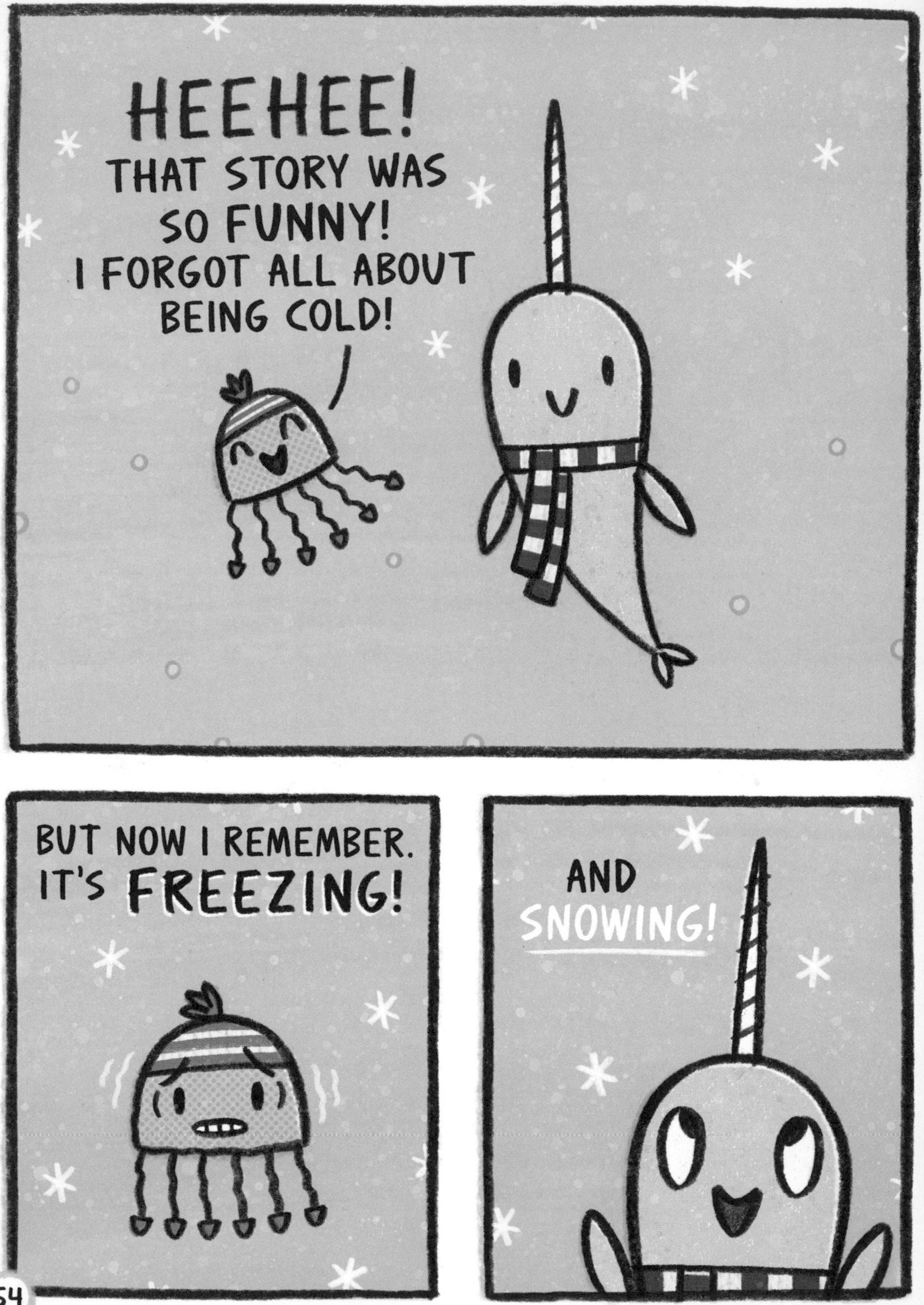
HEEHEE! THAT STORY WAS SO FUNNY! I FORGOT ALL ABOUT BEING COLD!
BUT NOW I REMEMBER. IT'S FREEZING!
AND SNOWING!

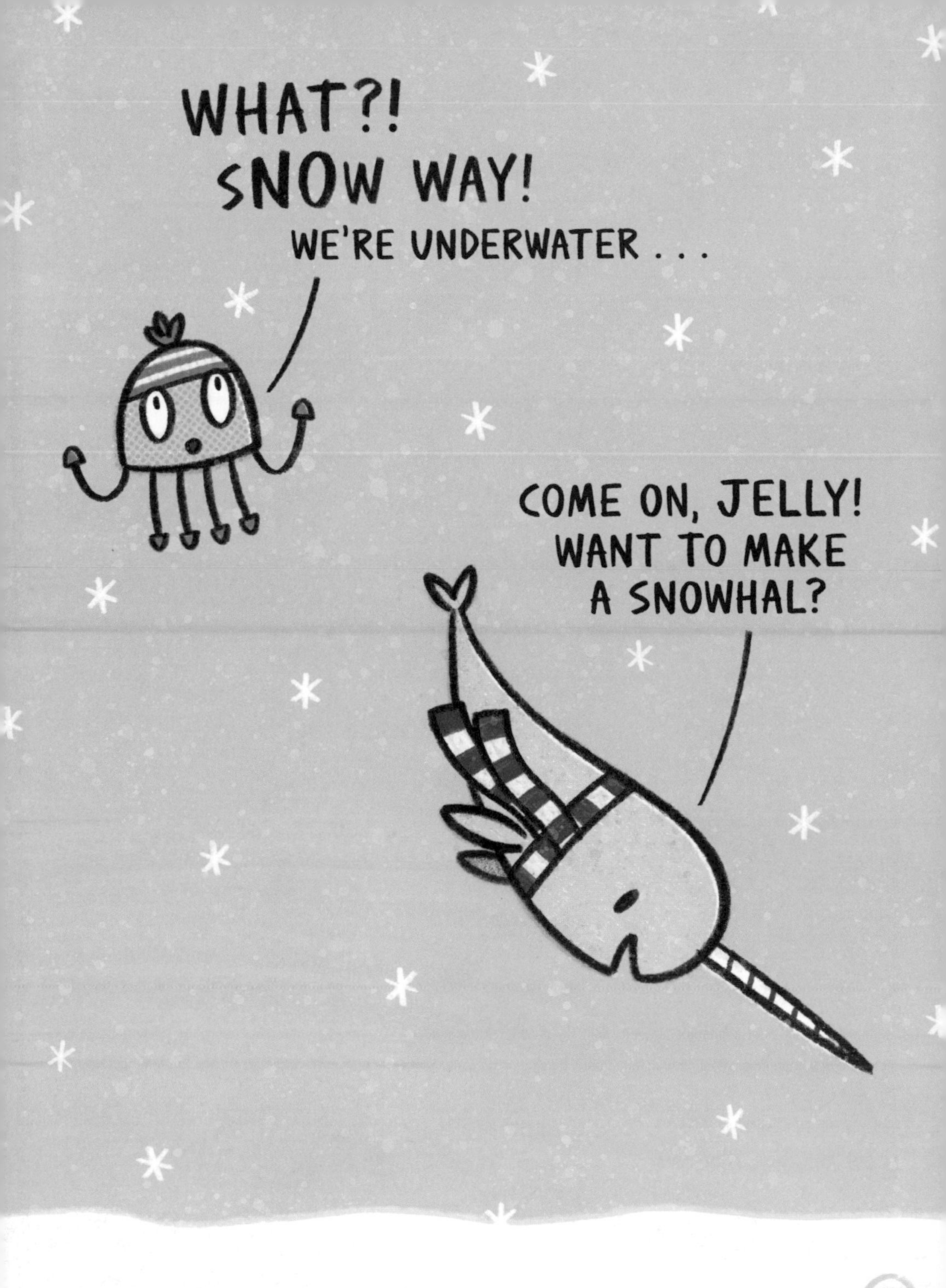
WHAT?! SNOW WAY! WE'RE UNDERWATER . . .
COME ON, JELLY! WANT TO MAKE A SNOWHAL?

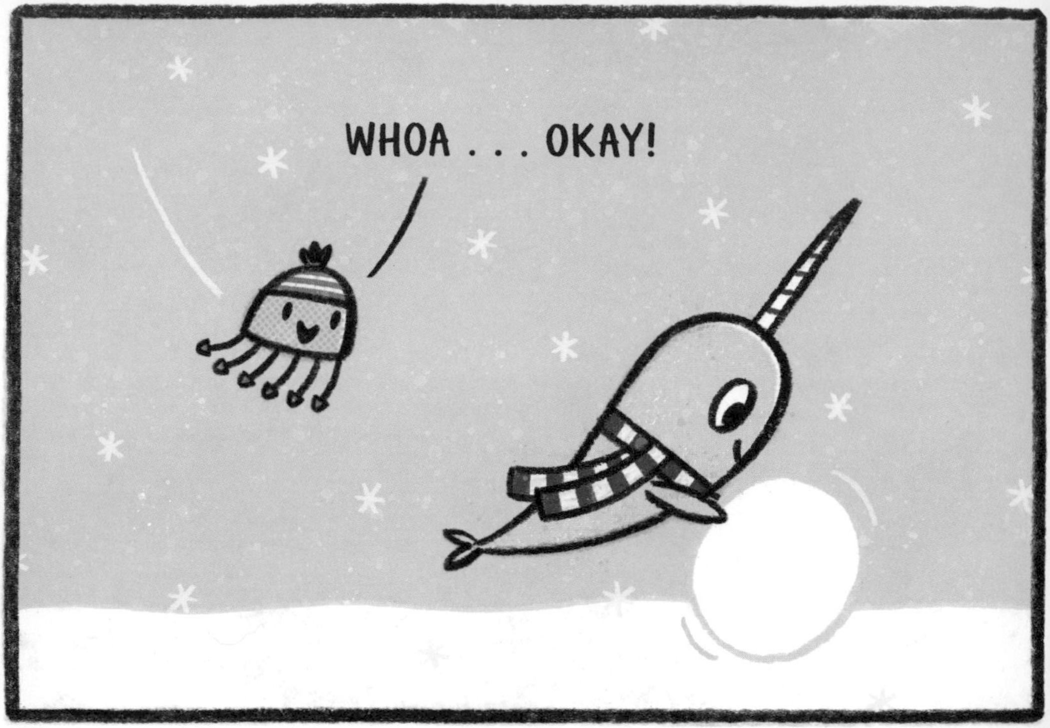
WHOA . . . OKAY!

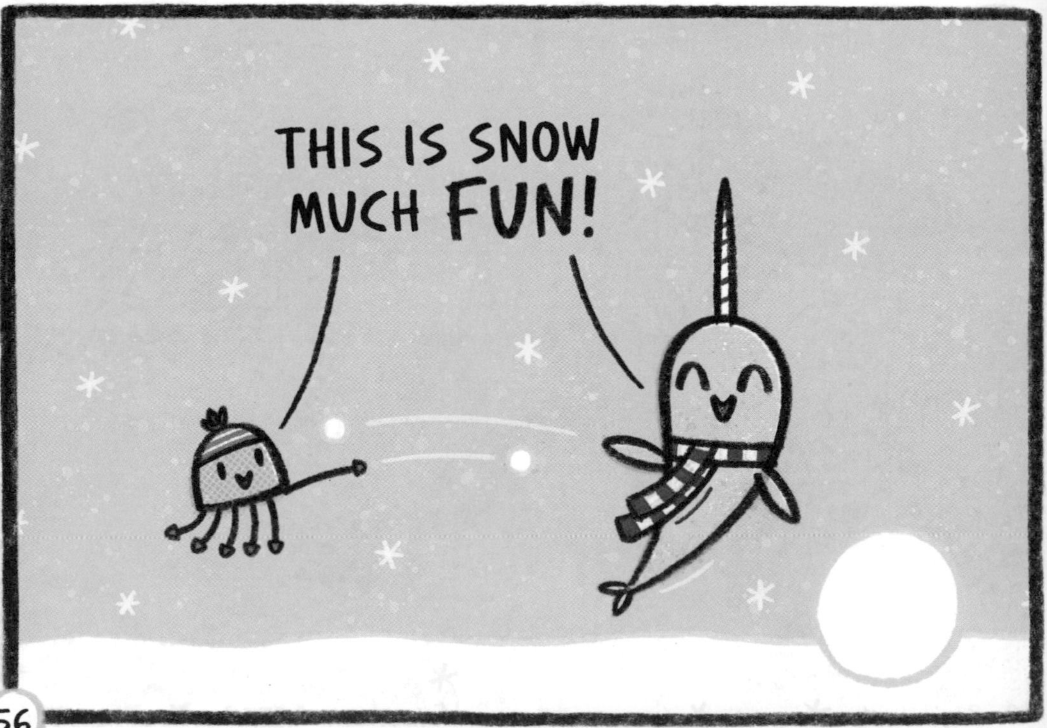
THIS IS SNOW MUCH FUN!

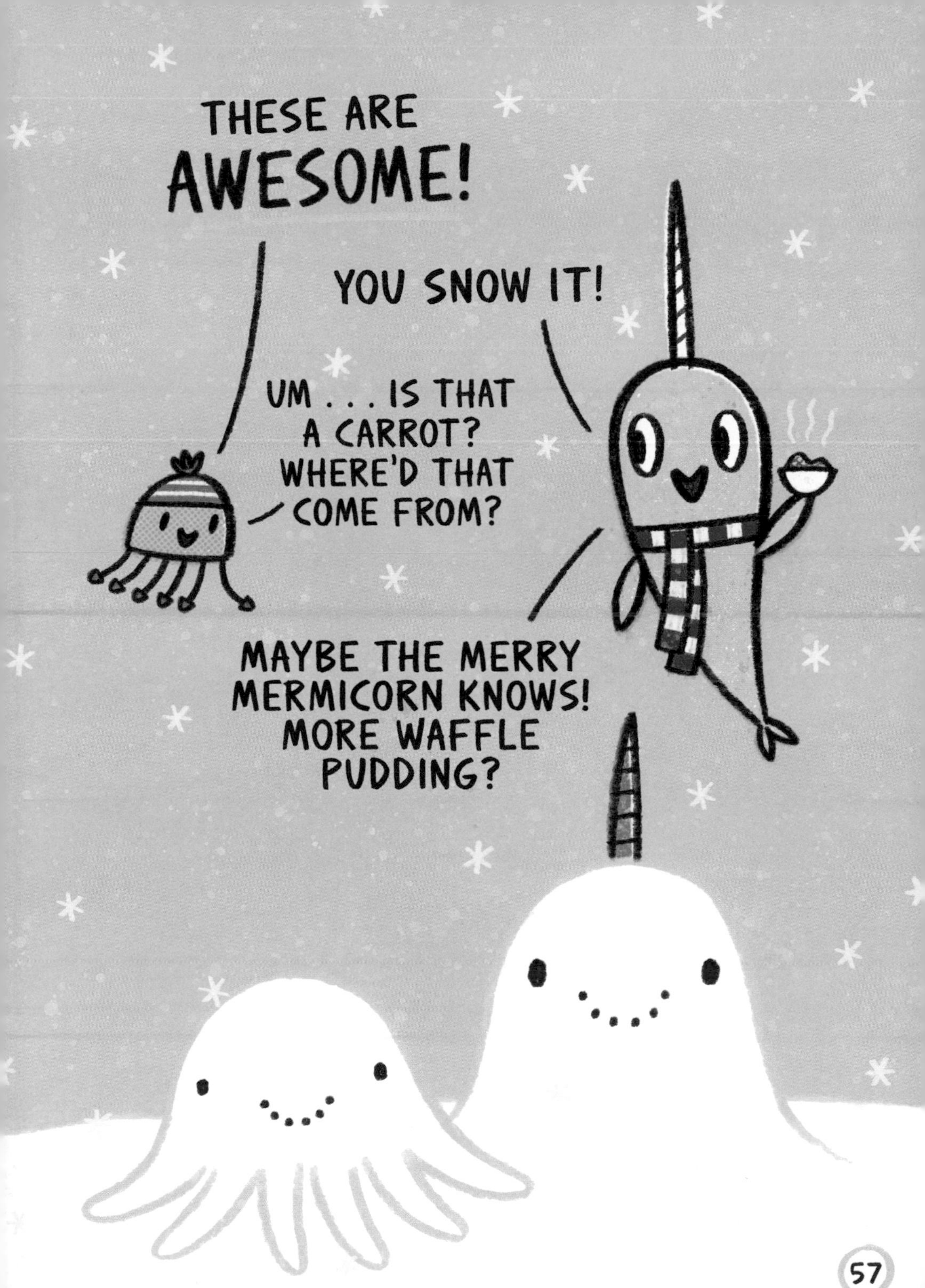
THESE ARE AWESOME!
YOU SNOW IT!
UM . . . IS THAT A CARROT? WHERE'D THAT COME FROM?
MAYBE THE MERRY MERMICORN KNOWS! MORE WAFFLE PUDDING?

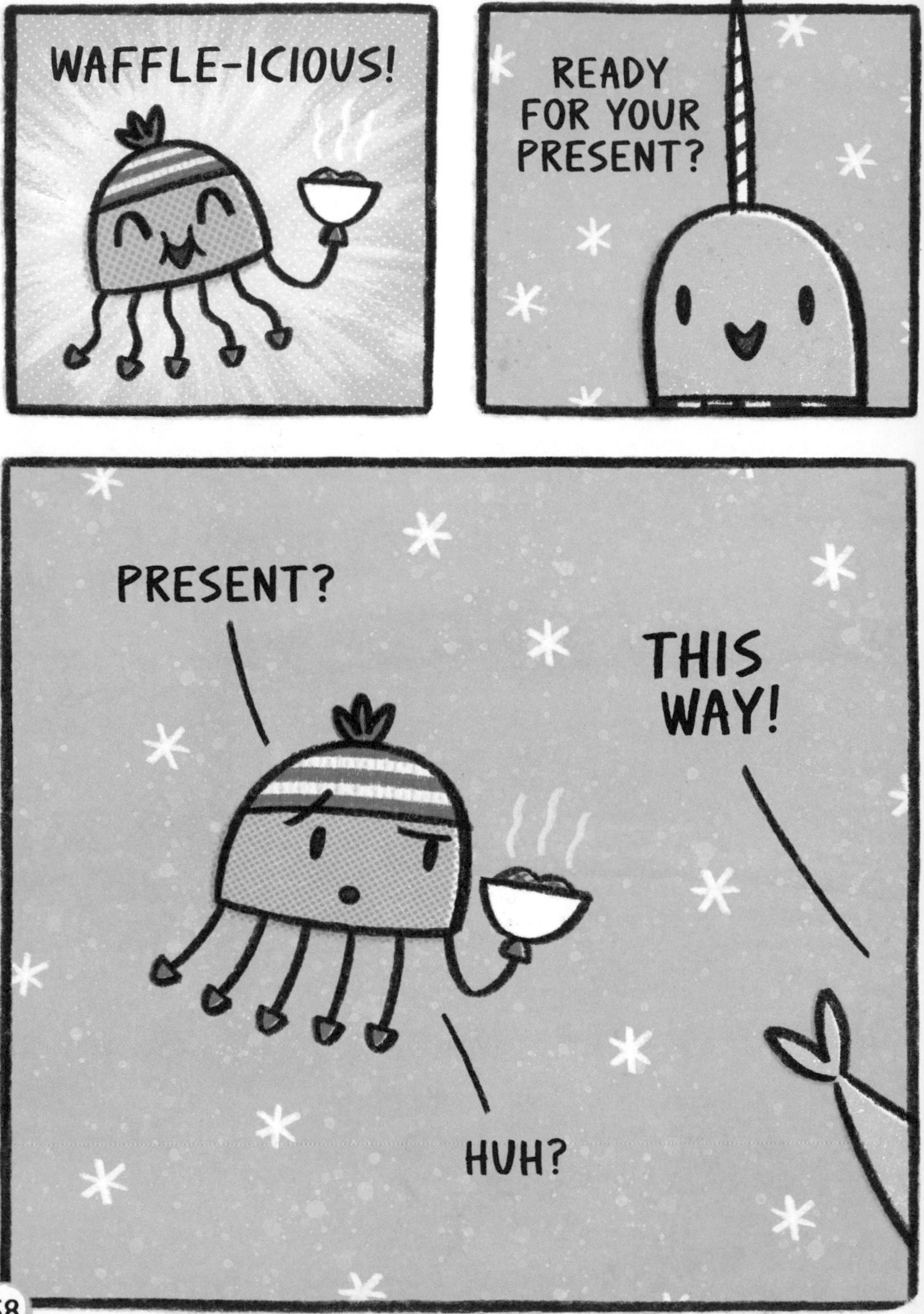
WAFFLE-ICIOUS!
READY FOR YOUR PRESENT?
PRESENT?
THIS WAY!
HUH?

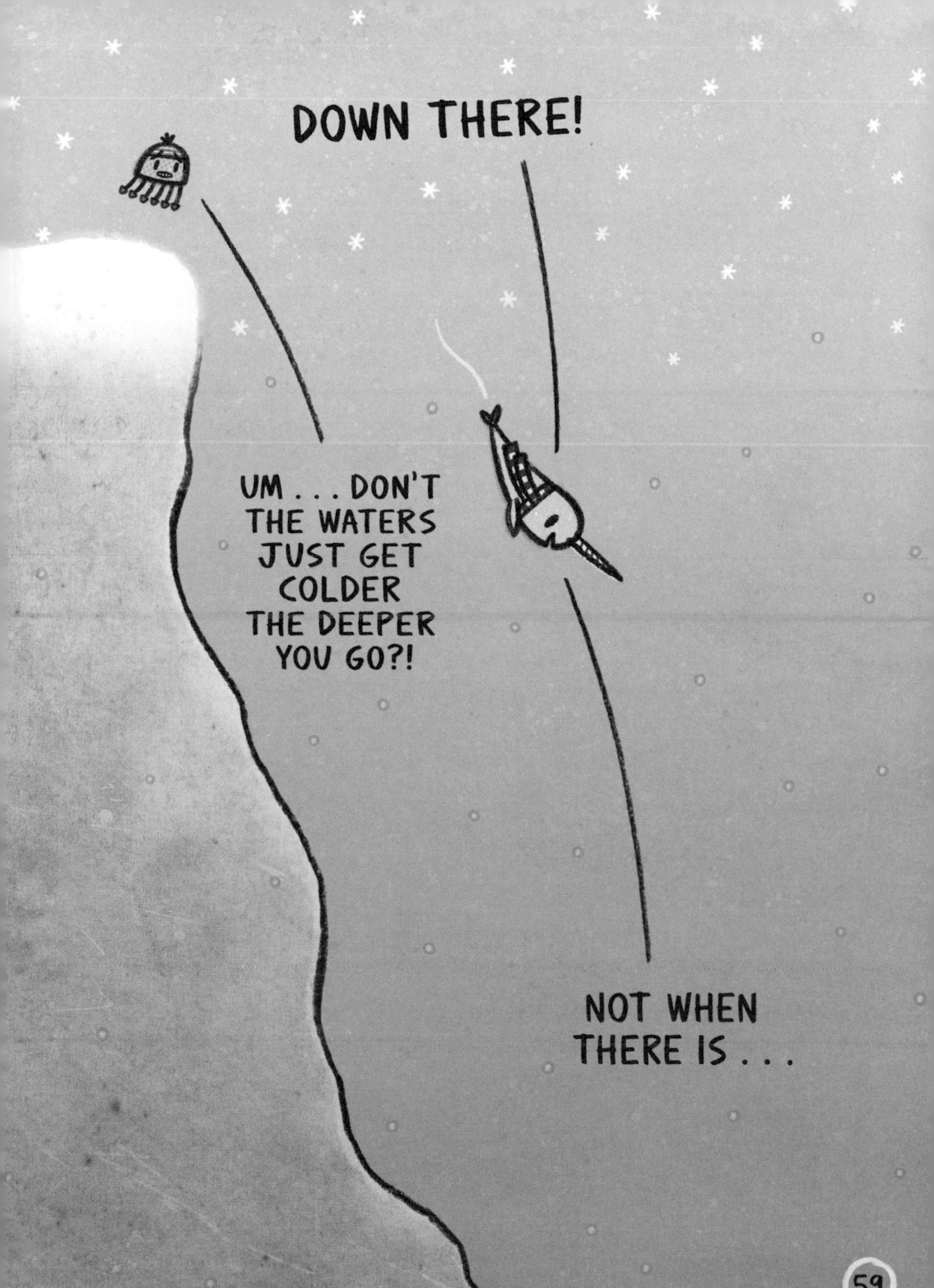

DOWN THERE!
UM . . . DON'T THE WATERS JUST GET COLDER THE DEEPER YOU GO?!
NOT WHEN THERE IS . . .

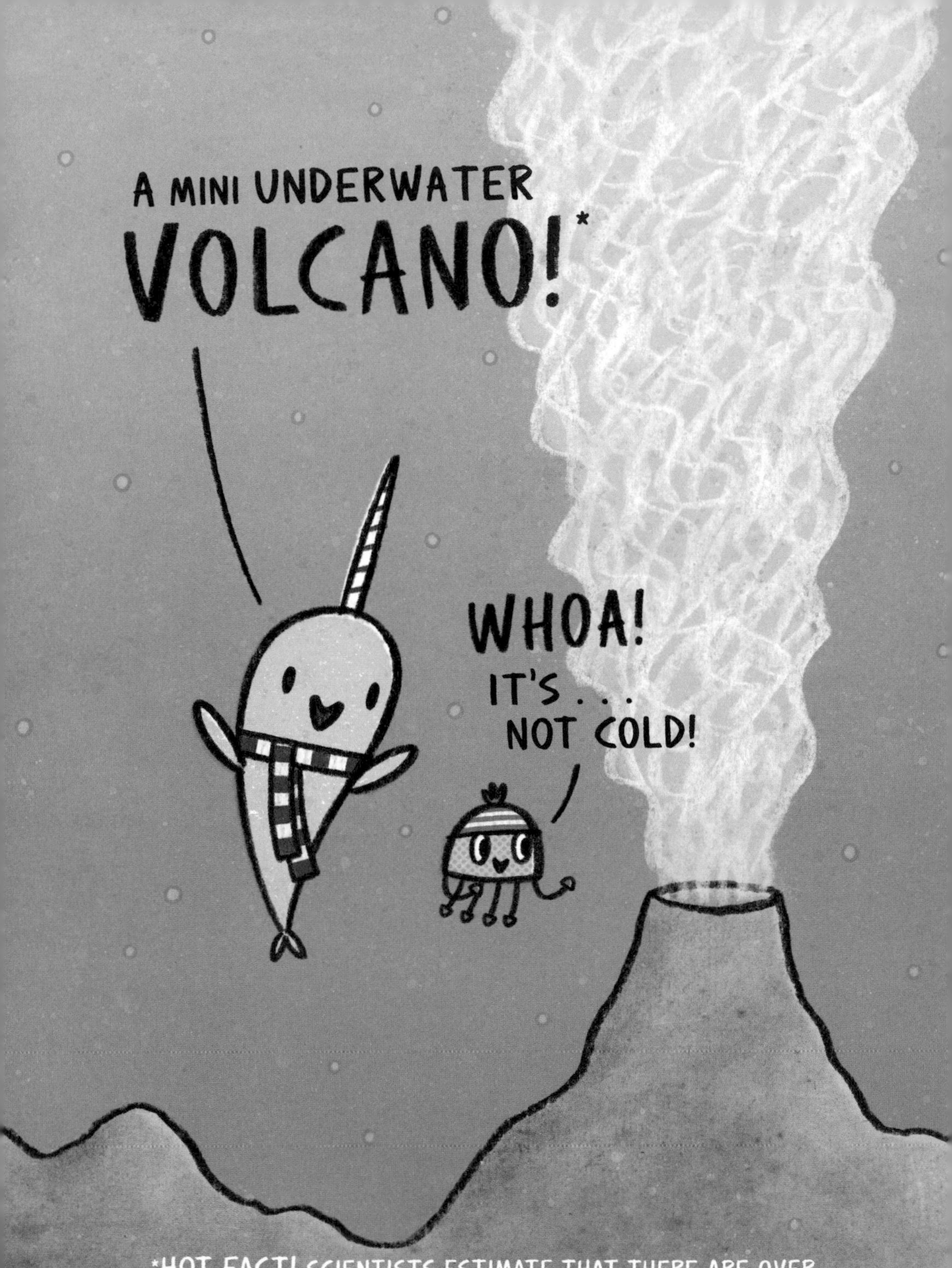
A MINI UNDERWATER
VOLCANO!*
WHOA!
IT'S . . .
NOT COLD!

*HOT FACT! SCIENTISTS ESTIMATE THAT THERE ARE OVER A MILLION SUBMARINE VOLCANOES IN THE WORLD!

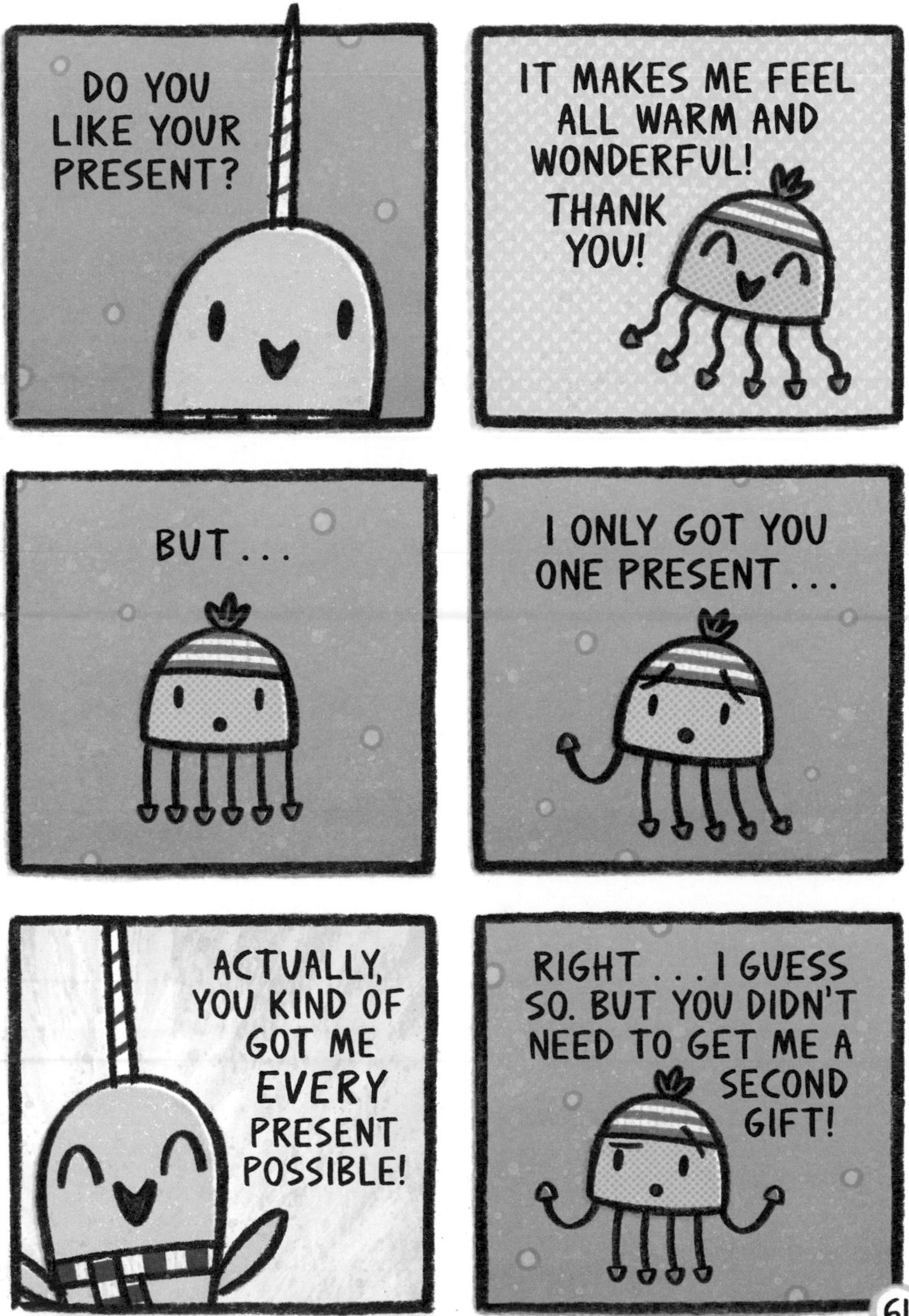
DO YOU LIKE YOUR PRESENT?
IT MAKES ME FEEL ALL WARM AND WONDERFUL!
THANK YOU!
BUT . . .
I ONLY GOT YOU ONE PRESENT . . .
ACTUALLY, YOU KIND OF GOT ME EVERY PRESENT POSSIBLE!
RIGHT . . . I GUESS SO. BUT YOU DIDN'T NEED TO GET ME A SECOND GIFT!

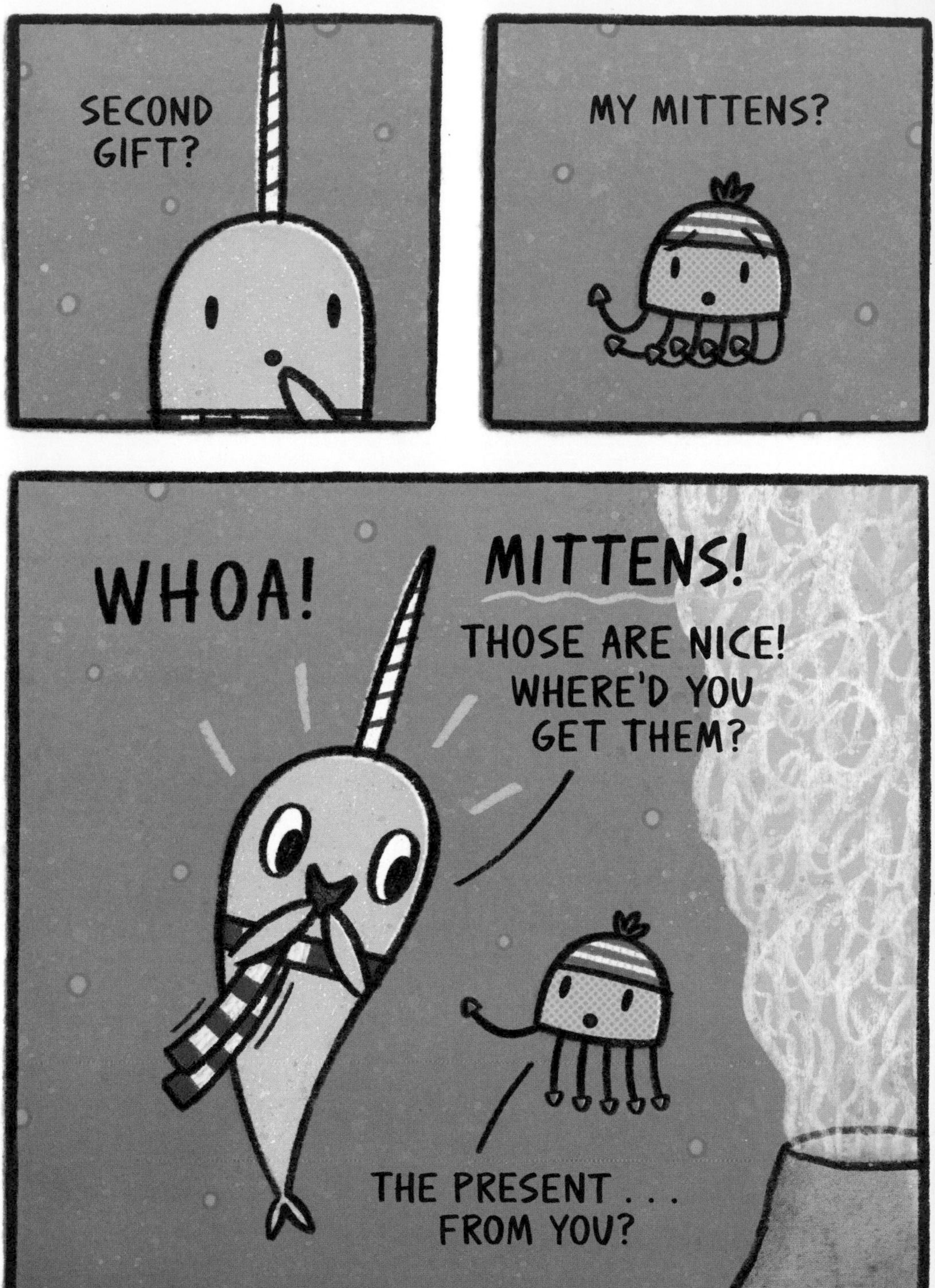
SECOND GIFT?
MY MITTENS?
WHOA!
MITTENS!
THOSE ARE NICE! WHERE'D YOU GET THEM?
THE PRESENT . . . FROM YOU?

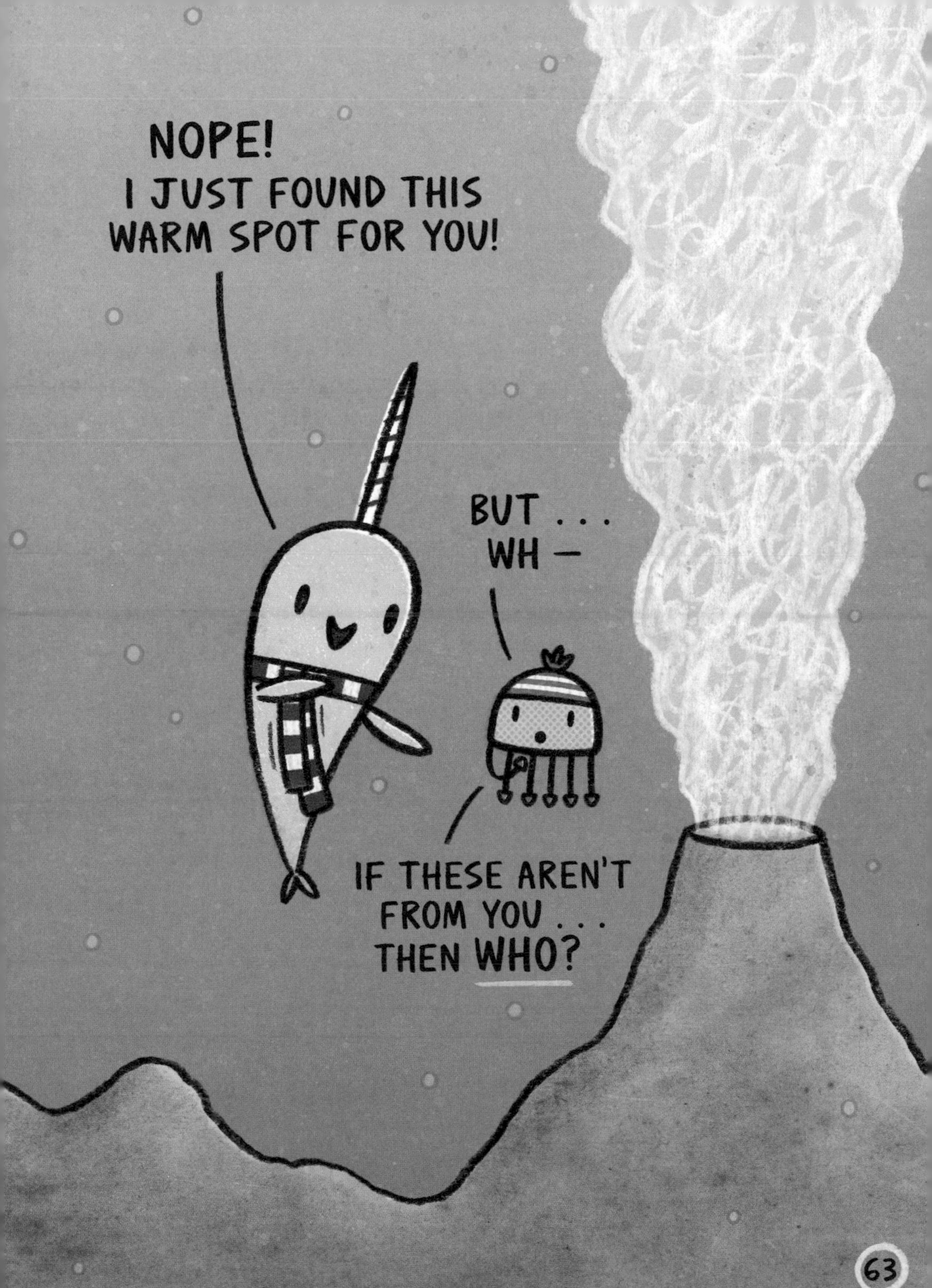
NOPE!
I JUST FOUND THIS WARM SPOT FOR YOU!
BUT . . . WH —
IF THESE AREN'T FROM YOU . . . THEN WHO?

Happy Narwhalidays!

THE MERRY MERMICORN

SONG!

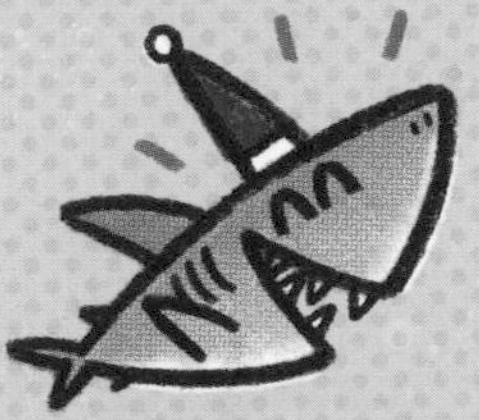

WE FISH YOU A MERRY MERMICORN,
WE FISH YOU A MERRY MERMICORN,
WE FISH YOU A MERRY MERMICORN,
AND SOME BUBBLY GOOD CHEER!

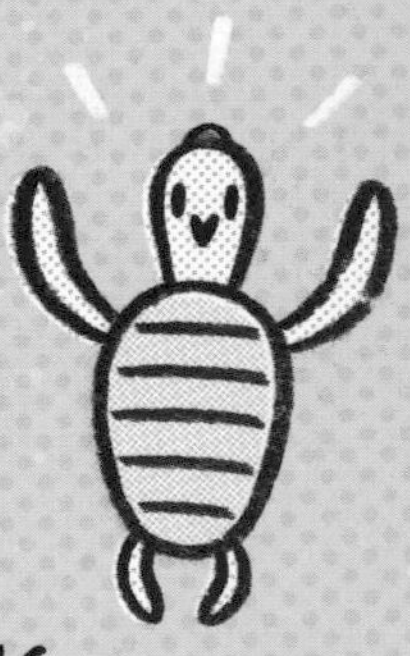

GOOD TIDE-INGS WE BRING
TO YOU AND YOUR FIN;
WE FISH YOU A MERRY MERMICORN
AND SOME BUBBLY GOOD CHEER!

NOW BRING US SOME WAFFLE PUDDING,
NOW BRING US SOME WAFFLE PUDDING,
NOW BRING US SOME WAFFLE PUDDING,
NOW BRING SOME OUT HERE.

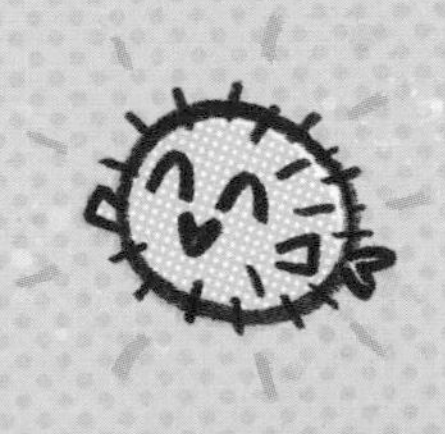

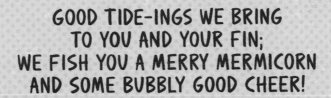

GOOD TIDE-INGS WE BRING
TO YOU AND YOUR FIN;
WE FISH YOU A MERRY MERMICORN
AND SOME BUBBLY GOOD CHEER!

WE WON'T GO UNTIL WE GET SOME,
WE WON'T GO UNTIL WE GET SOME,
WE WON'T GO UNTIL WE GET SOME,
SO BRING SOME OUT HERE.

GOOD TIDE-INGS WE BRING
TO YOU AND YOUR FIN;
WE FISH YOU A MERRY MERMICORN
AND SOME BUBBLY GOOD CHEER!

WE FISH YOU A MERRY MERMICORN,
WE FISH YOU A MERRY MERMICORN,
WE FISH YOU A MERRY MERMICORN,
AND SOME BUBBLY GOOD CHEER!

NARWHAL, I SUPPOSE THIS IS A WAFFLEY WONDERFUL SEASON AFTER ALL!

BUT NEXT YEAR . . . LET'S SWIM SOUTH FOR WINTER.

MORE NARWHAL AND JELLY

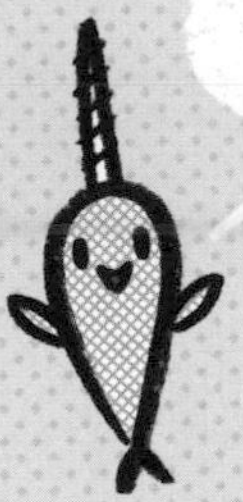

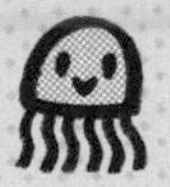

ADVENTURES COMING SOON!

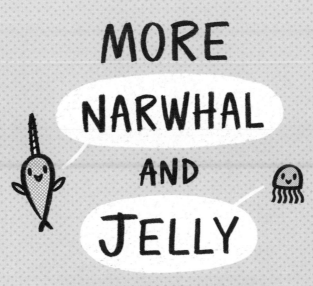

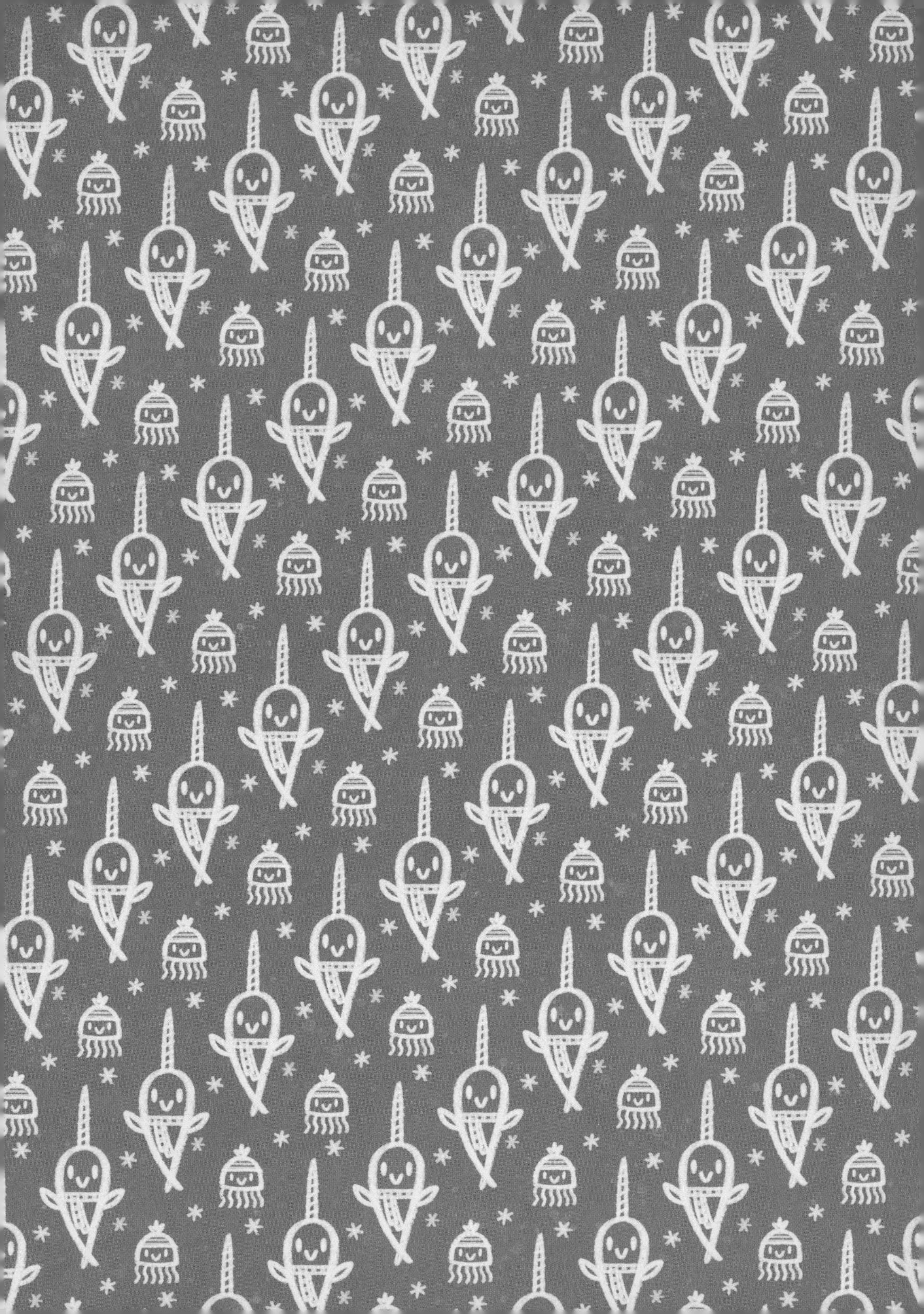